UNDERCOVER
IN THE
UNDERWORLD

Who can you trust?

The truth is out there…

ON THE RUN 3

UNDERCOVER IN THE UNDERWORLD

GORDON KORMAN

■SCHOLASTIC

First published in the UK in 2007 by Scholastic Children's Books
An imprint of Scholastic Ltd
Euston House, 24 Eversholt Street
London, NW1 1DB, UK
Registered office: Westfield Road, Southam, Warwickshire, CV47 0RA
SCHOLASTIC and associated logos are trademarks and/or registered trademarks
of Scholastic Inc.

First published in the US in 2005 by Scholastic, Inc.,
Text copyright © Gordon Korman, 2005
The right of Gordon Korman to be identified as the author of this work
has been asserted by him.
Cover illustration by David Wyatt, 2007

10 digit ISBN 0 439 94388 4
13 digit ISBN 978 0439 94388 8

A CIP catalogue record for this book is available from the British Library

Printed and bound by Bookmarque Ltd, Croydon, Surrey
Papers used by Scholastic Children's Books are made from wood grown in
sustainable forests.

1 3 5 7 9 10 8 6 4 2

This is a work of fiction. Names, characters, places, incidents and dialogues are
products of the author's imagination or are used fictitiously. Any resemblance to
actual people, living or dead, events or locales is entirely coincidental.

www.scholastic.co.uk/zone

For Jon Batchelor,
Web guru and friend

1

Dear Mom and Dad,

First things first: we're fine. You don't need to know where we are.

Don't worry about us. You should be thinking about yourselves right now. You're the ones who are in prison for a crime you didn't even commit. Just hang on. Believe this – we're going to prove you're innocent. Every breath we take is dedicated to that. It's the only thing that matters.

Don't listen to the lies the FBI tells you. We didn't burn down Sunnydale Farm, even though no place ever needed a good fire more than that one. Anyway, it serves them right for sticking us on a prison farm just because our parents were in jail. It's true that we've broken the law a few times since then, but only when there was no other way. Nothing is more important than staying free so we can clear your names.

That's all for now. As you can guess, we don't have a ton of time for letter writing. One last thing: we saw

1

you on TV. Please stop asking us to turn ourselves in. It's not going to happen.

We never stop thinking about you. . .

Fifteen-year-old Aiden Falconer signed his name and then slid the letter in front of his eleven-year-old sister, Meg. "Stop it," he said gently. "If Mom and Dad see tears on the paper, they'll think we can't handle it."

She sniffled, but her tone was strong. "We're running for our lives, our last name has turned into a synonym for terrorist, and on top of it all some bald wacko is trying to kill us. Mom and Dad have PhDs. They can probably guess we're a little freaked out."

Aiden leaned back in his seat at the secluded corner table. The food court wasn't crowded, but a fugitive could never be too careful. In the past few days, their pictures had been on CNN and in *USA Today.*

That's the problem with the outlaw business, he reflected nervously. *Success works against you. The longer you stay ahead of the cops, the more famous you become. And celebrities get noticed.*

Meg scribbled her name, and Aiden folded the letter and sealed it in the envelope. The address sickened them — their father, at the McAllister Maximum Security Correction Facility in Florida. They hoped he would have a chance to share it with Mom at a women's prison not far away.

"Come on," he said. "Let's get to the gate."

"Aren't you going to mail it first?"

Aiden shook his head. "Airports have their own postmarks. When this letter shows up at the jail, we don't want the cops to know we got on a plane in Providence. Then they could check airline records to see where we went."

They were travelling under fake names, of course. But the tickets had been purchased online using their mother's SkyPoints on Trans-Atlantica Airlines. The government had seized the Falconer family's home and had frozen their bank accounts and assets. All that was left were their frequent-flier miles. Mom had always travelled under her maiden name, Louise Graham. That meant Aiden and Meg could use the points without using the name Falconer, which was as well known as that of any sports hero or movie star . . . for all the wrong reasons.

Falconer equalled traitor, betrayer, terrorist. Husband and wife criminologists, convicted of aiding and abetting enemies of the state.

And these days, it also equalled fugitive. As they

ducked and dodged the FBI, the juvenile authorities, and dozens of local police forces, the Falconer children were becoming every bit as notorious as their parents.

Aiden felt every eye in the concourse boring into him. This was the scariest part of being a fugitive. The danger was invisible until it was too late.

Until somebody's dialling 9-1-1. . .

The agent checked their boarding passes and examined their school IDs. These had been purchased just the day before from a joke shop near Harvard University in Massachusetts. The cards identified them as Gary Graham and his little brother, Eric.

Meg wasn't thrilled about pretending to be a boy. But the blow to her pride was still a thousand times better than getting caught. In a pharmacy toilet, Aiden had used a sideburn trimmer to buzz her hair down to a crew cut. Scowling into the mirror, even Meg had been forced to admit she was a dead ringer for a boy of eight or nine.

Their scam: the police were looking for a brother and sister, not two brothers. It wasn't perfect, not by a long shot. But it just might get them on this plane. At fifteen, Aiden was too young to hold a driver's licence but old enough to accompany a younger sibling without parental consent forms. They had done research to make sure of that.

The security checkpoint. Aiden took a deep breath. Whatever went wrong, it was going to happen right here.

As they'd rehearsed, the Falconers turned and waved goodbye to the crowd of total strangers assembled outside the entrance to the gates. They didn't know any of the people, of course. But it looked much more natural for two kids to have somebody seeing them off.

Meg passed through the metal detector first, and Aiden followed.

Beeeep!

The guard approached him. "Please empty your pockets, sir."

Aiden fought down a wild desire to turn tail and run. *Calm down, idiot! You have nothing to hide.*

But the truth was, Aiden and Meg had everything to hide. Especially if the guard happened to notice who the letter was addressed to.

Carefully, as if handling nitro, Aiden placed the envelope face down in the plastic basket.

The next item in his pocket was almost as dangerous. It was a nine-year-old faded photograph of a family friend named Frank Lindenauer. "Uncle" Frank had been their parents' CIA contact. He was the one person on earth who could prove that John and Louise Falconer were innocent of treason and had been working for their own government the whole time.

Face down, he repeated to himself, slipping it under the letter.

The last item, placed carefully on top of the other two, was a change-of-residence confirmation from the California Department of Motor Vehicles. The address on it was Aiden and Meg's only clue to where Frank Lindenauer might be found.

His stomach knotted like a pretzel, Aiden watched his family's entire future disappear into the X-ray machine. He waited until the basket had safely emerged on the other side before stepping back through the metal detector.

Beeeep!

He nearly hit the ceiling. What was going on here? Could this machine somehow read his guilt? His fear? Was it picking up the machine-gun rhythm of his hyperactive heart?

It turned out to be much simpler than that. The guard reached around and pulled something out of

Aiden's back pocket. Aiden stared. It was the metal pen they had used to write the letter.

"That should help," the woman said with a slight smile.

There was a smattering of applause from the line up of passengers when Aiden made it through the detector without incident.

"Way to keep a low profile," snickered Meg when they were side by side on the moving sidewalk.

Classic Meg. She could laugh off a near miss like that. But not Aiden. Not with the stakes so high.

This was what their lives had become. This was the new reality — hanging by the narrowest of threads over a pit of disaster. One misstep, one unlucky break, and they were back in custody. Who would search for Frank Lindenauer then?

It would be the end of all hope for Mom and Dad.

A pen! A lousy fifty-cent pen!

Any chance of a future for the Falconer family could crumble over something as insignificant as that.

Minneapolis, Minnesota.

Not their destination, not yet. But the trip to Los Angeles included a plane change here, with a two-hour layover between flights. It was the perfect opportunity for the Falconers to mail their letter in a non-airport mailbox.

Meg gazed out the window of the taxi, enjoying the view. Minneapolis seemed like a nice place, dotted with parks and small lakes. It reminded her of her own neighbourhood.

Not any more, she thought bitterly. Her last view of the Falconer home had featured fluorescent yellow crime-scene tape and a padlock from the Department of Homeland Security.

And Mom and Dad being handcuffed by a cop the size of an NBA power forward.

Agent Emmanuel Harris – J. Edgar Giraffe. It was a funny nickname for a very unfunny person. Harris was the man who had ruined all their lives.

I wish I could see the look on his face when that letter shows up postmarked Minnesota.

The thought of Harris and his FBI cronies tearing Minneapolis apart for two fugitives who were in California put a satisfied smirk on Meg's face all the way back to the airport.

They had no problem re-entering security, and boarded the plane for their connection to Los Angeles.

It was over the Badlands of South Dakota that Meg noticed the flight attendant staring at them.

"Excuse me, but do I know you kids? You look *so* familiar."

"We fly a lot," Meg replied readily. "We're constantly winging it to LA to visit our dad."

Meg was a smooth liar – a useful skill for a fugitive. Her brother had book smarts, but he couldn't live by his wits the way she could.

"That must be it," the steward said dubiously. "You've probably been on this flight before." He didn't look convinced.

As the journey progressed, the young man continued to cast frowning looks in their direction.

Typically, Aiden was ready to panic. "He isn't buying it," he whispered anxiously. "He definitely recognizes us, and he knows it isn't from some flight."

"Take it easy," Meg soothed.

But it was difficult to follow her own advice. If the flight attendant made the connection between their faces and the Falconer fugitives, he could radio airport security in Los Angeles. There was no escape from a plane, which had only one door for hundreds of passengers. She and Aiden would be trapped like rats on a Boeing 757.

At last, the seat-belt sign came back on. Meg peered out the window at the vast city below, sprawling from the ocean to the desert. There was only one word to describe it – humongous. Finding one person in LA would be like searching for a needle in a haystack.

If he's even in LA. . .

Meg didn't allow herself to breathe again until the wheels of the plane had lurched on to the runway. California. She'd never thought they would make it this far.

It happened in the first-class cabin as they waited in the long line to exit the flight. A businessman pulled his briefcase from the overhead luggage compartment. The clasp came undone, and a folded newspaper fell on to the seat.

Meg gawked. The tabloid was open to a screaming headline:

NOW YOU SEE THEM, NOW YOU DON'T! FALCONER KIDS ESCAPE POLICE A SECOND TIME

In the centre of the page were two photographs – the Department of Juvenile Corrections mugshots of Aiden and Margaret Falconer.

There was a gasp of recognition from the flight attendant. He looked from the siblings to the newspaper and back again.

The Falconers' eyes locked, the message passing between them as if by radar: *Get off this plane!*

But how? We're packed in like sardines!

Meg reached up and yanked a small suitcase from the overhead rack. She swung it in a reckless arc, trying to clear some space around her. The passengers ducked and leaned out of the way.

"Hey, watch it!" complained the businessman as the carry-on smacked him.

He wheeled to face his attacker, and Meg deftly sidestepped him. When he reached for her, she dropped to the floor, scrambling on all fours through the obstacle course of purses, computer bags and legs.

Aiden was too tall to follow her. He grabbed hold of the overhead rack and swung himself to seat 1B.

"Stop those kids!" ordered the steward.

The gate agent grabbed Aiden at the door. At knee level, Meg snatched a briefcase off the carpet and slammed the brass corner on to the woman's foot.

"Ow!"

In the chaos, Meg clambered up beside her brother and hauled him out on to the bustling jet bridge. It was packed, with a second flight emptying from the other side.

It's too crowded! she thought desperately. *We'll never get away from all these people.*

There was only one other exit – a door at the end of the jetway. They burst through it and found themselves on a metal platform fifteen feet above the busy tarmac of LAX airport.

Aiden started for the rickety ladder. Meg was about to follow when she saw it – a small tractor pulling three open luggage carts. It was about to pass right below them.

Her brother swung a leg over the side, but she froze him with a single syllable: "Jump!"

"What?"

"Jump!" And before he could stop her, she stepped off the platform.

"*Meg!*" he howled in dismay.

At first she thought she'd mistimed her leap, that she was about to plunge fifteen feet to hard pavement and broken bones. But as she fell, the tractor veered left to avoid an orange cone, bringing the three carts into perfect position. She landed in the middle trailer, bouncing like a rag doll off a stack of garment bags. The back of her head struck the metal clasp of a valise, and she saw stars.

Fighting through the pain, she looked up just in time to see Aiden drop into the rear cart. He hit the pile of suitcases with a muffled *Oof!* and burrowed, a mole tunnelling through a mountain of luggage. Meg did the same. The tractor chugged on, its driver completely unaware of his two hitchhikers.

The flight attendant ran out of the jet-bridge door, yammering into a mobile phone. "Of course I know where they are! They're right over –"

He scanned the tarmac in disbelief. Not fifteen seconds before, the Falconer fugitives had been right before his eyes.

He thought back to the newspaper headline: NOW YOU SEE THEM. . .

Where had they gone?

Aiden pressed his face into the soft side of a duffel. The thumping of his heart in his ears drowned out the roar of the baggage tractor. Desperately, he tried to calm himself to the point of rational thought:

1. We're in an airport.

2. Airports are packed with security people.

Any way he tried to twist it, the conclusion was the same: if he and Meg were spotted, a well-trained high-tech army would descend on them. They wouldn't stand a chance.

His stomach still churned from the leap off the platform. Meg was fearless.

I have enough fear for the two of us, Aiden figured.

All at once, the bright sunlight dimmed. Aiden peered between the pieces of luggage. They had entered some kind of warehouse. He hoisted himself up by the rim of the cart and risked a look out. The tractor navigated a dark, cluttered structure with suitcases stacked all around. Several trailers were parked at the far end, where uniformed agents unloaded bags on to conveyer belts.

We're in the guts of the baggage claim!

In the cart behind him, Meg's head surfaced between backpacks. Aiden gestured for her to stay down. But they couldn't hide for ever. In a few minutes, somebody was going to be unloading these carts.

Can we make it back outside?

Difficult, he decided. The warehouse was full of baggage handlers. And with each passing second, the tractor pulled them further away from the only exit—

No, wait – there's another way out of here!

A simple hand gesture was all it took to transmit the plan to Meg. One advantage of life on the run – the Falconers had become experts at silent communication. It was the telepathy of desperation. They were constantly trapped, constantly fleeing. Escape had become second nature.

Aiden held up three fingers. Meg nodded – three seconds. The siblings did the countdown together: three . . . two . . . one. . .

At the same instant, they vaulted out of the carts and hit the cement floor running.

"Hey, you're not allowed back here!" barked an angry voice behind them.

"Now!" Aiden cried.

They sprung on to the baggage conveyer. Aiden hit the moving rubber, somersaulted, and righted himself just in time to see three airport employees sprinting towards them. The belt carried them through a divider of hanging canvas straps into the baggage retrieval system.

The passage was narrow, and he whacked his head on a low-hanging bar. Plastic rollers buffeted them on both sides. Ahead they could see hydraulic plates and rotating wheels designed to keep bags from getting stuck.

"Is this safe for people?" Meg called over the mechanical racket.

"Safer than getting caught." But in truth, Aiden had his doubts.

Suddenly, the belt deposited him on a slick metal chute, and he was sliding. He burst through another canvas divider to see the teeming arrivals level of Los Angeles International Airport. People stared as he hit the circling carousel, stumbled unsteadily to his feet, and jumped to the floor. A split second later, Meg came sailing down the chute. He yanked her off the baggage claim, his heart soaring.

We're out!

No sooner had the thought crossed his mind than an earsplitting siren cut the air.

They barrelled through the automatic sliders, propelled by the terror of their worst fear coming true. In thirty seconds, LAX would be locked down and searched. Escape had to be now or it would definitely be never.

Then he saw it: the Hertz Rent-A-Car courtesy bus, parked at the kerb directly in front of them. The open doors beckoned like a lifeboat to a drowning pair.

They bounded on to the step an instant before the doors folded shut. In the rearview mirror, they caught a glimpse of the driver's questioning eyes on them. Meg defused that with a wave into the crowded interior. "It's OK, Dad. We made it."

Seven minutes later, they were pulling into the Hertz lot, the wailing of the airport alarm now out of earshot. As the other passengers lined up at the rental counter, the Falconers hailed a passing taxi and jumped inside.

"Where to?"

Aiden unfolded the DMV letter and read the address. "One-fourteen Cabrini Court, Venice Beach."

Meg slumped back in the seat, suddenly too weary

to hold herself upright. "Well, how do you like California so far?"

If he hadn't laughed, Aiden was pretty sure he would have burst into tears. Constant danger, non-stop pressure, non-stop terror – it should have been old news by now.

He was discovering that you never got used to it.

Three thousand miles away from Venice Beach, Agent Emmanuel Harris of the FBI entered the luxurious dark-panelled lobby of the Royal Bostonian hotel in Boston, Massachusetts.

He was an imposing figure, standing six feet seven inches tall, holding a Starbucks hot-cup – size venti, just like Harris.

He crossed the lobby in three expansive strides and showed his badge to the uniformed desk clerk. "Aiden and Margaret Falconer stayed here. I want to know—"

"Spell that, please," the woman interrupted.

"The Falconer kids!" Harris exploded. "They're fugitives, wanted by half the government. You think they registered under their real names?"

The clerk was flustered. "I – I didn't – I'll get the manager."

Harris took another sip and wondered how it had

all gone wrong. A year ago, he'd been a national hero, bringing the most notorious traitors in half a century to justice. Doctors John and Louise Falconer, the criminologists who had lent their expertise to terrorists. A slam-dunk case.

The Falconers claimed to have been working for a CIA agent named Frank Lindenauer. But Lindenauer had disappeared off the face of the earth — if the man had ever existed in the first place. The result: life sentences for the Falconers, and a big promotion for Harris.

Yet Harris had got something else out of the deal — sleepless nights. What if the husband and wife college professors had been telling the truth? In that horrible scenario, not only were two innocent people suffering in prison, but their children were on the run like hunted animals for no reason.

And it's all my fault.

The manager hurried over. "What seems to be the trouble, sir?"

Harris flashed his ID once more. "I'm here about Aiden and Margaret Falconer."

"Ah, yes — they left the hotel on Monday without checking out. Registered under Graham, I believe." The man tapped the keyboard expertly. "Here it is. Louise Graham."

Harris recognized the name immediately. "Louise Graham is in a maximum-security prison in Florida. How could she possibly pay for a five-star hotel room in Boston?"

"She didn't," the manager replied. "Our records say the three-night stay was purchased over the Internet with SkyPoints from Trans-Atlantica Airlines."

Harris was thunderstruck. "Frequent-flier miles?" The FBI had frozen the Falconers' financial assets. But frequent-flier points?

Clever. No, not just clever – *brilliant*. His grudging respect for those resourceful kids went up a notch.

He flipped open his mobile and dialled his assistant in Washington, DC. "I need you to access a Trans-Atlantica SkyPoints account for me. The name is Louise Graham. Give me all the recent activity."

There was a long pause on the line. Even the FBI needed special authorization to access a private company's customer records. "OK, I've got it," the reply came finally. "In the past week, I see an award deduction for a deluxe long weekend at the Royal Bostonian hotel—"

"I'm there right now," Harris said impatiently. "Anything else?"

"Two airline tickets. The flight lands . . . whoops, it landed a few minutes ago."

Harris could feel his heart thudding in his chest, something that happened when he drank a lot of coffee, which was always. "Landed where?"

"California. LAX."

Harris wasn't sure whether to curse himself for losing the Falconers in Boston or hoot with glee that they were back on the radar screen. "I'm on my way to the airport. Book me on the next flight. And get some local agents to check LAX *immediately*."

"Should I instruct the airline to freeze the frequent-flier account?" his assistant asked.

"No, but put a tracer on it. If anybody uses those miles, I want to be the first to know." He hung up and turned to the manager. "Thanks for your help."

"We always co-operate with the police," the man said primly. "I gave the same information to the other detective."

Harris froze. "Other detective?"

"He was here just this morning. You know, your office should really get its assignments straight so you don't waste manpower posing the same questions to the same people."

"Describe him," Harris demanded.

"He was large — although not as large as you.

Quite muscular. Oh, yes, and his head was shaved completely bald. That was his most striking feature."

Emmanuel Harris felt his blood chill inside his veins. It was him – the unidentified bald male suspect. He had police ID, but he was no cop.

He was out to harm Aiden and Margaret Falconer, possibly even kill them.

But why? The parents were the traitors, not their kids.

There was no time to waste on speculation. If Harris knew about the frequent-flier miles, the bald impostor might do, too. He was probably on a plane to California already, hours ahead of the FBI.

Harris rushed out of the hotel and hailed a taxi with a skyscraping wave of his arm. It was now doubly important to arrest Aiden and Margaret Falconer.

It could be the only way to save them.

114 Cabrini Court was a three-storey stucco apartment house just inland from the surf shops and tourist traps that lined Venice Beach. It was a well-kept place, with hibiscus bushes by the door and flower boxes along the broad balconies. The paint was fresh, if a little too pink.

The taxi drove away, leaving the Falconers looking up at the building.

Meg could barely raise her voice above a whisper. "Do you think there's a chance that the real Frank Lindenauer is in there?"

Her brother squared his shoulders. "Only one way to find out."

They entered the vestibule, and Aiden pressed the buzzer above mailbox 2C.

A woman answered in an Eastern European accent Aiden couldn't place. "Yes, who is this, please?"

Aiden took a stab at it. "Mrs Lindenauer?"

"What?" The voice was blank. "Mrs Who?"

Meg jumped in. "We're looking for Mr Lindenauer. Mr Frank Lindenauer."

"You come to the wrong place. No Mr Frank here."

"He *used* to live there," Aiden explained. "Uh – did you know the person in the apartment before you?"

"No – I don't know nothing." The click over the intercom indicated that the conversation was over.

Aiden let out a breath. "So much for the lucky break."

Meg was furious. "I didn't come three thousand miles for 'I don't know nothing'! Somebody has to remember this guy."

Before Aiden could stop her, she rang every doorbell on the board. There were a few voice replies before one unwary soul buzzed them in.

They started with their quarry's former neighbours on the second floor. There were a couple of not-homes and a pair of Japanese exchange students who couldn't even pronounce Lindenauer, let alone recall meeting him. The young woman in 2D didn't recognize the name or the photograph, and she had been living there for three years.

"He was probably gone before you moved in," Aiden concluded.

A man with an armload of groceries appeared and dropped his parcels in front of the last door in the hall. "Are you talking about the Harpers from 2F? They moved back east about five years ago. We had a block party the day they left and took that parakeet with them."

"What about Lindenauer?" Meg asked urgently. "Frank Lindenauer."

The man frowned. "Don't know any Lindenauer..." And then light seemed to dawn. "You're not talking about the Phantom? Big guy — red hair, beard. Lived in 2C."

Aiden stepped forward eagerly. "You knew he worked for the CIA?"

The man gawked. "Did he really? We were just kidding! We called him the Phantom because he was so weird. He came and went at all hours, disappeared for months at a time. A real nut-job about privacy, too. Wouldn't even put his name on the mailbox."

"When did he move away?" Meg asked.

"Who could tell? He was never really here. The only person he ever talked to was the super. You should ask him — apartment 1A."

The super instantly recognized the photograph. "Oh, *that* guy! Yeah, I remember. Frank somebody."

"Do you have any idea where we can find him?" asked Aiden.

The man shrugged. "He paid his rent on time, that's what mattered to me. And always in cash. The tenants were afraid of him – thought he was in the mob or something. You can call the management company to see if he left a forwarding address. But that would be five, six years old."

The let-down was so intense the Falconers could almost taste it. Sure, they didn't think it would turn out to be as simple as knocking on a door and having Lindenauer answer it. But they hadn't expected the trail to be so cold.

The super sensed their disappointment. "He's a relative of yours?"

"Our father," Meg lied, flashing saucer-wide tragic eyes. "He and Mom lost touch when I was just a baby."

"Wait – I think I've got something for you." The super disappeared into the apartment and returned a moment later with a dusty shoebox. *2C* had been scribbled in Magic Marker on the masking tape that held the lid in place. "It's just a few odds and ends your old man left in his place when he moved out.

26

I'd been saving it for him, but, hey – you're his flesh and blood, right?"

"We sure are," confirmed Meg.

The way she said it, no one would have doubted it for an instant.

Venice Beach attracted a wide variety of people, from LA's hippest hipsters to tourists in Hawaiian shirts and cheap sunglasses, from combat-booted punks to aging hippies who looked like Gandalf.

The Falconers sat on a bench by the bike path, poring over the contents of the shoebox — which were every bit as bizarre and mismatched as the motley crew riding and Rollerblading past.

There was a deck of cards, a doorstop, a wrapped bar of soap from the Oriental Hotel in Bangkok, a high school ring, a lady's hoop earring, three shirt buttons, a dainty pair of opera glasses, the shell casing from a .32 calibre bullet, a handful of coins from Malaysia and the Philippines, and a small brass key bearing the number 347.

Meg was crestfallen. "Just a bunch of old junk."

"Come on, Meg," Aiden chided. "Didn't you learn anything growing up in a house with two criminologists? There's a ton of information in this box."

Her eyes flashed anger under a frown. "You're not talking about criminology. You're talking about Dad's books."

In addition to his career as a college professor, Dr John Falconer was also the author of a series of detective novels. His hero, Mac Mulvey, had an uncanny ability to find clues in other people's cast-offs.

"Look," Aiden continued, "a hotel in Bangkok, money from Malaysia and the Philippines – that proves he travels, especially in Asia."

"We *know* that already – the neighbour just told us he was never home. The earring – we know he had a lot of girlfriends. The bullet – we know he's CIA. What's left? The ring – so he has fingers. Eureka."

"Take a look at that key," Aiden insisted.

She shrugged. "A suitcase key."

"I don't think so. There's no brand name or logo. And the number – 347. This is a locker key."

Meg was instantly on board. "And if a CIA agent thinks something is so important that it isn't safe in his apartment – that he has to lock it up someplace else—"

"Then it has to be big stuff," Aiden finished. "Maybe even something about Mom and Dad."

"So we've got the key," his sister said excitedly. "All we need to do is find the lock that it opens."

Aiden stared at her. Meg could go from the depths of depression straight up to the stratosphere in the blink of an eye. Her idea of "all we need to do" completely boggled his mind. In a city of millions of people, with who knew how many bus stations, train stations, airports, shopping malls, swimming pools and public beaches, it was not going to be a piece of cake to find the right locker 347.

It was dusk, and at that moment, the street lights over the pathway came on, growing to full brightness. Aiden was surprised to see a mark on the key he hadn't noticed before. He held it directly under the lamp and examined it closely. Near the key-ring hole, four tiny letters had been engraved in the metal: SMRC.

"SMRC?" Unsure of his own eyes, he handed it to Meg. "What do you make of this?"

And when he looked away from her, a scene straight out of a TV movie of the week was unfolding not five feet in front of him.

A lanky teenager with razor-short hair and a goatee stood at a beachside shop, holding up a baggy

T-shirt. A shorter, stockier teen in a Dodgers jersey seemed to trip on thin air and stumble into the first boy. As he fell, the clumsy newcomer reached a hand into his pocket.

A click. The glint was unmistakable. Street light on metal.

A switchblade!

Aiden was never sure why he did it – only that the reaction was instantaneous and almost automatic. With a warning cry of *"Knife!"* he launched himself forward and rammed his shoulder into the *g* in *Dodgers*.

The attacker was knocked back, staggering into a table of bathing suits. He sprang up again, brandishing the blade in front of him. In a chilling reality check, Aiden took full account of the terrible mistake he'd just made. He had picked a fight with a knife-wielding city kid when he himself had no means of defence.

The first slash missed the tip of his nose by an inch and a half – so close he felt wind as the blade sailed past. He wanted to run, but in his overpowering dread, his legs wouldn't respond to instructions from his brain. He was turned to stone, waiting for the burn of cold steel slicing into him.

Amazingly, it wasn't fear of the pain that stoked

his terror. It was the thought of leaving his gallant little sister alone and unprotected. She was a tiger, but she was still only eleven.

I'm sorry, Meg! I did the best I could!

He braced himself for the strike . . . and then Dodgers Jersey wheeled and fled.

Huh?

The boy with the goatee and two other teens flashed by in hot pursuit. One of them upended a sale rack of sunglasses. Tourists screamed, and the shop owner burst out of the door, hurling curses.

Aiden watched in a mixture of fascination and horror as Goatee and the newcomers chased Dodgers Jersey through the narrow lane between storefronts, leaping over garbage cans and discarded boxes.

A late-model Mustang convertible screeched to a halt in the roadway at the end of the alley. Without missing a stride, Dodgers Jersey vaulted over the rear door, landing in a heap in the back seat. The car peeled away.

Meg appeared at Aiden's side. "What are you, nuts? What did you do that for?"

The scene was bedlam. Spectators flooded to the shop, where dozens of pairs of sunglasses were scattered about the wreckage of the broken rack. The owner was scrambling around, trying to recover his merchandise, dialling 9-1-1 on a mobile phone. A little kid who had been knocked over in the chaos was crying. His mother dabbed at his skinned knees with a wet napkin while his father raved about how the neighbourhood was going to the dogs.

Sirens wailed in the distance — Aiden's second unpleasant surprise of the past minute. He had done nothing wrong. In fact, his actions had been heroic, if risky and stupid. But face time with the cops was the last thing a fugitive needed.

Especially not on a day when we've been spotted busting out of the Los Angeles airport.

He grabbed the shoebox from his sister, tucked it under his arm, and began pushing her through the gathering crush of people.

Meg wanted answers. "What's going on? Why did you bodycheck that guy?"

"Not now," he muttered through clenched teeth.

Once clear of the crowd, he ran, towing Meg by the arm. They dashed along the bike path and ducked into one of the side alleys, zigzagging inland via short residential streets. It was only when they were well in from the water, lost in the spiderweb of the Venice Beach grid, that Aiden slowed to a fast walk.

Meg scrambled to keep up on her shorter legs. "Come on, Aiden," she panted. "Tell me what happened!"

"I think —" he was in a daze, but he didn't interrupt his stride — "I think I just stopped a murder."

@leaves.net, the famous Venice cyber tea shop, saw its clientele change several times each day – bodybuilders early, artists in the afternoon, businesspeople after work, and college students late. Very few school-age kids turned up for *@leaves.net*'s combination of designer teas and Internet access. But that night around ten p.m., what appeared to be a teenager and his younger brother were hunched over a monitor, ignoring a cup of steaming Earl Grey.

Meg snorted in disgust. Younger brother! She didn't mind so much pretending to be a boy – even an eight-year-old.

But I miss my hair!

She pounded the keyboard, accessing another chunk of Louise Graham's frequent-flier miles. Mom had more than seven hundred thousand Sky-Points – the fruit of years of worldwide travel on the lecture circuit. It would be enough to book Aiden and Meg hotel rooms for a long time.

A wave of sadness froze the mouse in her hand. *A long time.* At his-and-hers maximum-security prisons in Florida, Mom and Dad were serving his-and-hers life sentences. Nothing else qualified as "a long time".

Meg pointed to the screen. "How about this place? The Beverly Palace Hotel and Spa."

Aiden was in the process of divvying up the contents of the shoebox between their pockets. "Let's chuck the doorstop. But the opera glasses might come in handy. Like mini binoculars."

Meg was absorbed in her research. "Check it out — the spa has hot bubbling mud wraps. What's a hot bubbling mud wrap?"

"That car has passed by here before," he said suddenly.

"Huh?" She glanced up from the screen. Her brother's attention was now focused out the window at the passing traffic.

"That El Camino — you know, that old-fashioned clunker with a car front but a flatbed in back like a pickup truck. Watch, it'll come around again."

Sure enough, a few minutes later, the El Camino idled into view. The paint appeared to be orange and brown — very 1970s. Although it was impossible to make out much detail, four dark silhouettes were clearly visible — two in the cab and two in the flatbed.

Aiden and Meg huddled behind the monitor until the vehicle had traversed *@leaves.net*'s picture window and disappeared down the block.

"You think it's the cops?" Meg whispered. "In an El Camino?"

Aiden's brow furrowed. "Undercover agents? FBI maybe?"

Meg couldn't picture Emmanuel Harris in a 1970s macho mobile. On the other hand, it was hard to envision the agent's six-foot-seven bulk in anything smaller than an aircraft carrier. "If it isn't police, then who could it be?"

Aiden drew in a nervous breath. "For all we know, he's just circling the block looking for a parking space big enough for that monster. But I think it might have something to do with what happened on the beach."

Her eyes widened. "You mean the guy with the knife?"

He nodded. "LA is gang country. Regular people don't go around carving each other up with switchblades. I think I might have stuck my nose into some kind of gang war."

A gang war! Wasn't there enough danger in their lives already, being pursued across the country by the police, the juvenile authorities, the FBI, and Hairless Joe, a bald nutcase with a grudge? And now an LA street gang was mad at them? It just didn't seem fair.

"What are we going to do?" she asked anxiously. "We can't even call the cops!"

"The next time they drive by," Aiden said in a low voice, "we'll take off in the opposite direction. At least then we'll have a few minutes before they pass again and find out we've bolted."

Willing her fingers not to tremble, Meg shut down the Web browser. They waited, eyes riveted to the window, huddled so close that each could feel the other's heartbeat. No El Camino appeared.

Five minutes. Seven. Then ten.

"Maybe we were wrong," she suggested hopefully.

Her brother was stubborn. "I don't think we were wrong. And I don't think they went away, either."

Another ten minutes. Meg counted off the seconds, all six hundred of them, just to keep her mind occupied. She had never been big on waiting. She would rather face something – *anything* – just to avoid the fear that could consume her from the inside like acid.

Aiden was the opposite. Mr Patience – watching his inaction was enough to drive her nuts. He'd always been that way, even about something as harmless as a game of Monopoly. He could slow the pace to a crawl agonizing over whether or not to buy Marvin Gardens.

"Let's *go*," she urged.

Aiden thought it over a moment, then started for the door.

The instant they stepped on to the sidewalk they spotted it – the El Camino parked down the block. All at once, the lights came blazing on, fixing the Falconers in their blinding beams.

The hesitation was only one beat. They were off down the sidewalk, running full tilt. The car roared to unmuffled life and peeled into traffic after them.

Meg stumbled on the uneven concrete. Before she could fall, Aiden grabbed her arm and pushed her in front of him. No words passed between them. They just fled.

It took only seconds for the El Camino to catch up. Without slowing, Meg glanced to her side. It was an image out of every gang movie she'd ever seen. The drive-by shooting. The windows would roll down, the gun barrels would appear. . .

"This way!"

She wheeled Aiden around a corner, and they pounded down a narrow alley that led to nothing but darkness. It was like running in deep space, a track meet in black velvet. But at least the car could not follow them here.

A squeal of tyres was followed by a series of metallic crashes as the headlights caught up with them. The El Camino was *coming*, bare inches from either side, bashing garbage cans out of its way. The high beams cast the Falconers' shadows on the brick wall in front of them. They looked around frantically. No fences, no doorways, no windows.

No escape.

Aiden tried to pull Meg behind him, but she struggled her way out again and stood by his side. Whatever this was, they were going to face it together.

The El Camino did not slow. Terrified and helpless, they watched it come.

This is no drive-by, Meg realized in agony. They were going to be crushed.

The big front grille kept hurtling towards them.

In what she believed would be her last thought, Meg saw her parents in prison, receiving the news that both their children were dead, gruesomely murdered in a far-off city.

And then the El Camino screeched to a halt barely eighteen inches in front of them. A tall, slim figure rose from the flatbed, stomped its way over to the cab, and glared down at them from the hood.

"What do you want from us?" Aiden rasped, petrified.

That was when the Falconers identified the face that hovered above them. It was indeed someone from the beach earlier that evening. But not the attacker in the Dodgers jersey.

It was the teenager with the goatee.

He spoke to Aiden. "I've been looking all over for you, man! You saved my life."

7

Aiden gawked at the boy he had rescued. "We don't want any trouble. I just saw the knife and pushed that guy away. I wasn't trying to mix in."

A grin that showed dazzling white teeth bloomed at the centre of the circle formed by the goatee and moustache. The teenager hopped down into the cramped space between the El Camino's grille and the Falconers. "Back this boat up," he ordered. "You're crowding my friends."

Growling and snarling, the El Camino reversed about ten feet, allowing Aiden and Meg to peel themselves off the wall. Meg couldn't suppress a tremulous sigh of relief.

"Sorry about that," Goatee apologized. "Russian driver." He held out his hand. "I'm Bo."

Aiden shook it, looking like he was grasping a live cobra. "Uh, hi—"

"No, no, no." Another flash of teeth. "This is the

part where you tell me *your* names." He and Meg exchanged an awkward handshake.

Aiden fumbled briefly. Who was he today? "Gary – Graham," he managed finally, quoting his airline ticket identity. "This is my brother, Eric."

"Wrong again," Bo said pleasantly. "This is your sister, Erica." He scrutinized Meg. "If you want to pass as a boy, you'd better trim those eyelashes."

Aiden was struck dumb. Even Meg, who could always come up with the right lie at the right moment, had nothing to say.

Bo shrugged. "That's fine. If you want to be Gary and Erica, it works for me. My real name is Boaz. Come on, I'll introduce you to the crew."

"We have to g-g-go," Aiden stammered in a failed attempt to be casual. "We've got to get home."

"Don't lie to a liar, *Gary*. You've got nowhere to go."

"We do so," snapped Meg. "We just stopped for –" her face twisted – "tea."

"Listen," Bo told them, "I've been on the street a long time, and I know some things. If you had a home, you'd be in it right now, being tucked in by Mommy and Daddy. Now, you don't have to tell me what your deal is, because I'm not nosy. But if you refuse to kick back with my crew so I can thank you for saving my life – well, that would hurt my feelings."

Aiden and Meg exchanged an agonized glance. Exactly how dangerous this streetwise Californian might be, they could not know. But it was clear that Bo was not the sort of person who took no for an answer.

So it was that the Falconers found themselves backing out of the alley at fifty miles an hour in the flatbed of a souped-up El Camino.

"Hang on!" advised the flatbed's other passenger, a petite brunette. "Teebs is a great driver, but he thinks he's still in Moscow. I'm Viv," she added.

"Gary and Erica," Bo introduced them. "They're with us now."

It was not what Aiden and Meg wanted to hear.

Bo and Viv held hands for the entire wild ride, which took them to an oceanfront parking lot, up over the kerbstones, and on to the beach itself. In a blizzard of airborne sand, Teebs guided the El Camino to a secluded spot hidden behind the now-closed municipal changing huts. Aiden could make out four or five figures gathered around what looked like a small bonfire.

"Last stop," announced Bo. "Everybody out."

The Falconers clung to the sides of the flatbed. Neither moved. What was about to happen to them?

"Aren't you hungry?" Viv asked.

Aiden squinted into the gloom. The fire – it was glowing coals in an ancient hibachi. Someone ripped open a shrink-wrapped packet of supermarket hot dogs. They sizzled as they hit the rusty grill.

They're taking us to a barbecue?

"You can lie about your names," said Bo, "but you can't tell me you guys have eaten in the last twelve hours."

"We really should get going," Aiden began.

Meg had a different opinion. "Oh, man, does that ever smell good!"

It made the decision easy. With a precious and dwindling thirty-seven dollars in their pockets, the Falconers could not afford to pass up a free meal.

Meg, who had once considered becoming a vegetarian, blasted through three hot dogs in the blink of an eye. Fugitives were not finicky eaters. They ate whatever they could manage to get, and savoured every bite.

Even Aiden had to admit that a full stomach felt

great. But he almost choked on the bun when he heard his sister ask, "So are you guys, like – a gang?"

Bo thought this was hilarious. "I think of us more as an autonomous collective."

Derisive laughter greeted this announcement, and Bo was pelted with sand.

"Easy on the vocab lesson, man," growled a surly teen everybody called Zapp.

It was true that Bo was remarkably well-spoken for a street thug.

"We're the IC," Bo went on. "International Crew. We're all from different places. I was born in Israel, Viv's Canadian, Teebs grew up in Russia, and Mr Maurice Zapp is from Pocatello, Idaho."

"That's not another country," Meg pointed out.

"You're right," mumbled Zapp in a flat baritone. "It's another planet."

Aiden kept his mouth shut. In his opinion, there wasn't a heck of a lot of difference between a crew and a gang. When one of the members asked Bo, "Anything on for tonight?" Aiden was pretty sure the guy wasn't talking about going bowling.

"Chill out," Bo told him. "We have *guests*."

Bo was definitely the leader. And for now, he seemed like he meant the Falconers no harm. But the only difference between the International Crew and the juvenile offenders at Sunnydale Farm was the simple fact that these kids hadn't been caught yet.

We can't get away from here fast enough, Aiden figured.

Mom had a rule under the heading of good manners: you had to wait at least twenty minutes after a meal before taking off. He estimated that length of time and then stood up and stretched. "Thanks a lot, Bo, but we really should be moving on."

"Tell that to your sister." Bo pointed to where Meg was collapsed against Viv's shoulder, fast asleep.

Aiden reached out to shake her awake, but Bo grabbed his arm. "Not necessary. You guys can crash with us tonight."

"No—"

"Listen, I don't know what you're hiding from. But trust me, I've been there. And I know how much a few hot dogs and a safe place to bunk can mean. Let me help. If it wasn't for you, I'd be lying on that bike path, bled out."

Aiden drew in a long breath of salt air. Unbelievable. They were running for their lives, hunted by the law, menaced by a terrifying killer. . .

. . .and now they were the reluctant house guests of a Los Angeles street gang.

The house was just a few miles from Venice Beach, but Aiden could see they had entered an alternate universe. Street after street of peeling paint – a maze of identical two-storey shoeboxes that had seen better days, or maybe not. The funky and fashionable strip of real estate that hugged the coastline was now behind them.

Bo put an arm around Aiden's shoulders on the mostly dirt front lawn. "Welcome to our little piece of shrapnel off the American grenade."

"How many of you live here?" asked Aiden, watching the procession of IC members from three cars file up the cracked concrete walk. He couldn't help noticing Viv shuffling the half-asleep Meg along with an almost motherly air.

"It's more like our headquarters, but anybody's welcome to crash," Bo said, then added meaningfully, "especially if you've got nowhere else to go."

A notice posted on the front door declared: THESE PREMISES THE PROPERTY OF THE DEPARTMENT OF VETERANS AFFAIRS.

"Some guy bought the place on the GI bill," Bo explained, "and when he couldn't make the payments, he took off. Left everything – furniture, the works."

The front lock was broken. Bo swung the door wide and ushered the group inside.

The interior was somewhat more impressive than Aiden had expected. At least it was reasonably clean. The decor reminded him of the dorm rooms at the small college where his parents used to teach – beanbag chairs, obnoxious posters, cheap blankets tacked up as curtains.

It still beats jail, Aiden thought, fighting a wave of sorrow. He and Meg could only imagine the horrific conditions Mom and Dad were forced to endure in prison.

And speaking of jail. . .

"Aren't you afraid Veterans Affairs will send the police over to keep an eye on the place?"

Bo shrugged. "They haven't yet." He fixed Aiden with a piercing gaze. "You and your sister look like a couple of clean-cut kids. Why are the cops after you? What have you done?"

"The cops aren't after us," Aiden countered far too quickly.

"Oh, sure. On the bike path, you two got out of there twice as fast as I did when we heard the sirens."

"I don't like to get involved," Aiden offered lamely.

Bo raised his expressive eyebrows. "You put yourself into a guy with an open switchblade — I think that counts as getting involved."

Aiden was growing nervous under the pressure of this questioning. He certainly wasn't going to come clean to a total stranger.

But how long can I keep putting him off before he gets angry?

Bo had been good to them so far, but he was a *gang leader*. There was no question he was dangerous.

Aiden summoned his courage. "You said you weren't nosy."

Bo looked shocked for a moment and then burst out laughing. "Come on, Gary, you'd better get some rest. You're not thinking like a prudent man."

He led Aiden upstairs to a tiny spare room where Meg was wrapped in a blanket, snoring softly on a couch. A sleeping bag was spread out on the floor for Aiden.

It wasn't the five-star hotel Meg had almost booked on the Internet. But suddenly, that bedroll seemed like the most sumptuous accommodation in any palace on the planet.

I can't remember the last time I had a chance to lie down...

Aiden collapsed gratefully on to the threadbare fabric.

"If you need anything, just holler," Bo tossed over his shoulder.

"Mmm-hmm." Aiden rolled over on his stomach. All at once, a sharp pain in his thigh brought him back up to a sitting position.

What the—

He reached into his pocket. It was the key – the locker key from the shoebox of Frank Lindenauer's knick-knacks, pressing up against his skin.

"Bo?" he called.

The door opened, and the boy with the goatee leaned in questioningly.

"Do you know what SMRC stands for?"

Bo thought it over. "Not off the top of my head. Where'd you see it?"

"On a billboard," Aiden said with a yawn. "Good night."

He felt a twinge of guilt for all the lying but quickly pushed it aside. Lies were small potatoes compared with what an LA gang was probably capable of.

He ran his finger across the jagged teeth of the key. Did the mysterious locker 347 – wherever it was – hold the evidence that would prove the Doctors Falconer were innocent—

If they were innocent. . .

Aiden's entire body jerked in the sleeping bag as if he'd been racked with a sudden intense pain. It was his deepest secret fear – greater, even, than his fear of capture.

What if John and Louise Falconer were guilty?

How could they be guilty? They're patriots! That's why they were helping the CIA in the first place.

And yet the doubts would not entirely disappear. If Mom and Dad were innocent, why wasn't the evidence more obvious? The FBI had put dozens of investigators on this case. OK, maybe they hadn't been looking very hard after the arrests had been made. But what about the Falconers' lawyers? They had moved heaven and earth for their clients and had still come up empty.

And Aiden and Meg, whose very lives depended on the outcome – what had they found?

A key. A single key to we-don't-know-what.

Could that be because there was nothing to find?

The wave of rage was white-hot and instant. Rage at himself, for entertaining such terrible thoughts. He had never – not once – given voice to his doubts. There were two reasons for this. First, an illogical, superstitious belief that saying it out loud might somehow make it come true.

But mostly, Meg would rip my lungs out.

He regarded his sister sacked out on the couch. Meg had zero doubt. In fact, he was certain that the possibility of guilt had never even crossed her mind. The whole world was clear-cut for Meg – black and white, good and bad, innocent and guilty.

Loyal and disloyal.

I want to believe! Who could be better parents – better people – than Mom and Dad?

Yet where was it written that good people couldn't do bad things?

Aiden and Meg had journeyed thousands of miles and risked their lives again and again to get to the bottom of the Falconer case.

But when they found the truth, would they really want to hear it?

Aiden tossed and turned on the floor. His tortured dreams took him back more than a year to his last night in a sleeping bag.

March 7.

The day the world ended.

The day of the arrest.

With no close relatives, Aiden and Meg had spent that night with their father's cousin and his new wife, people they hardly knew. It would have been uncomfortable under any circumstances. But especially that day – torn out of school by the police, eleven hours at the precinct house, watching the video clip of Agent Harris arresting Mom and Dad replayed endlessly on Fox News Channel.

"It'll only be for a couple of days," Dad said over the phone. "The whole thing's a misunderstanding."

Nobody realized the true scope of the nightmare that had just begun.

Meg got the guest bed. Aiden's restless twists and

turns were relegated to a sleeping bag on the den floor. He could still picture the large uncurtained window – the blazing sun that jolted him out of haunted semi-consciousness the next morning.

He didn't just remember it – he *felt* it.

Not only the powerful sun streaming in through the panes, but the sound as well. A muted but excited babble.

A crowd?

He picked himself up, shaking loose stiff and twisted muscles – the full-body ache of a night on hardwood after an entire day of gut-clenching anxiety.

That discomfort was forgotten the instant Aiden got a look out the window.

The front lawn had disappeared to be replaced by a sea of humanity. Reporters, cameramen, sound engineers. Dozens of TV station mobile units clogged the road. A futuristic skyline of satellite dishes.

What's going on?!

He ran for the front foyer. The cousin's wife cowered at the glass sidelights, gaping at the press invasion.

She tried to stop him. "Aiden! No!"

He barely heard her as he pushed on past. This was a chance to help Mom and Dad. To tell the world what good citizens they were. That they couldn't possibly have committed treason.

He threw open the door and ran outside. The throng of reporters closed around him like a giant amoeba absorbing its food. He was buffeted by bodies and equipment. A cable wrapped around his legs. He would havè fallen, but the crush of people kept him upright.

Microphones came from nowhere. A blizzard of shouted questions.

"Did you know your parents were working for terrorists?"

"*No!!*" he howled, but the media onslaught prevented him from saying anything beyond that single syllable.

"Have you had any dealings with the HORUS Global Group?"

"When did you realize that the HORUS Global Group was funnelling money to anti-American extremists?"

"My parents worked for the CIA!" Aiden shouted into the firestorm. "Ask Frank Lindenauer! He knows everything!"

That was when the real screaming started.

Meg.

She launched herself out of the house like a missile. Unlike Aiden, who thought he could set the record straight, his sister had a simpler purpose in mind.

"Get out of here! *Leave us alone!!*"

She blasted into the media swarm with such force that the entire crowd moved. The microphones that were shoved in her face she merely swatted away. He watched in amazement as she wrenched the camera out of the hands of a two-hundred-pound technician, reared back, and smacked him in the side of the head with it. If Aiden himself hadn't been so agitated, he probably would have cheered.

But her voice – he had never heard such sounds from her before. Sharp staccato shrieks that sounded like high-pitched, hysterical laughter.

"Meg!" he shouted, trying to push through the crowd to comfort her.

But he could not budge the mass around him. He was stuck, imprisoned, not by steel bars like his parents but by tons and tons of reporters. Struggle as he might, he made no headway, wheezing in wasted effort as he listened to his sister's cries. . .

"I'm coming, Meg!"

Aiden tossed himself awake, bumping his head

on the armrest of the couch and scrambling to his feet.

No crowd. No media feeding frenzy. No Meg.

It all came back to him: LA. The "borrowed" house. The International Crew.

But I heard screams.

There it was again – an agitated yip, punctuated by the slamming of cabinet doors.

Meg!

Aiden burst out of the room and down the stairs. What was she saying?

"Hey, you've got Bisquick!"

Huh?

"You mean you've never made pancakes before?" More slamming. "There has to be a frying pan in this place somewhere."

By the time Aiden got to the kitchen, a cosy domestic scene was in progress. Meg had Viv spooning batter on to a skillet while Teebs mixed up a new batch in a plastic bowl. Two more IC members, T-Dog and Pharaoh, looked on with rapt interest.

"That's it, nice and round," Meg advised Viv. "Don't make them too big. They'll fall apart when you try to flip 'em." She looked up and noticed her brother for the first time. "Morning, bro. Hope you're hungry!"

He could have cheerfully strangled her.

Calm down, he soothed himself. *She can't know you've been reliving the worst day of both your lives.*

"Does anybody mind if I take a shower?" he asked aloud.

"Mmmm," murmured Viv, concentrating on her pancakes like a diamond cutter evaluating a million-dollar stone.

Aiden climbed back upstairs and headed down the hall to the bathroom. No towel, no soap, no clean clothes. He was three for three. All the same, a shower was going to feel good. Then Meg could clean up, too, and they could get out of here before she was appointed Official Breakfast Chef to the Criminal Element.

He'd always envied his sister's ability to make friends easily. But this was ridiculous.

On the other hand, Bo and his "autonomous collective" had showed them a decent amount of kindness and hospitality.

I just hope we get out of here before we meet their dark side.

He pushed open the bathroom door and froze. There, standing over the counter, was Zapp. In front of him was a tower of crisp fifty-dollar bills.

He was counting out stacks of twenty, fastening each with a rubber band.

None of the fifties were faded or crinkled. It was perfect, brand-new money.

Aiden's heart skipped a beat.

Counterfeit money.

"Oops, sorry—" He attempted to back out.

An iron grip closed on the front of his shirt and hauled him inside. The bathroom door slammed behind him.

Zapp got right to the point. "If you ever, *ever*, tell anybody about this—"

"It's none of my business!" Aiden exclaimed quickly.

He was shoved hard up against the door. "*What's* none of your business?"

"Nothing!" Aiden stammered. "I didn't see anything! I was just going to use the shower."

Zapp looked at him with eyes that would have bored twin holes through titanium. Then he held out a stack of bills. "Take this."

Aiden moved his hands away. "Oh, no, I don't—"

"Grab it for me," Zapp commanded. "Now – put this on." He plucked a rubber band from the pile and handed it to Aiden.

Gingerly, as if the rubber were radioactive, Aiden slid the elastic on to the bundle of cash.

"Thanks, kid." Zapp peeled a fifty off the top of the tower and stuffed it into Aiden's pocket.

"What – what's that for?"

The reply was a vicious smile. "Now you work for me."

"No!" Aiden exploded. "I mean, no offence, but—"

"Bo's got a thing about funny money," Zapp explained. "It's federal – heavy heat. But if I go down, you're my partner. So keep your mouth shut. Got it?"

Aiden certainly did get it. Bad enough he was a fugitive. Now he had graduated to counterfeiter.

10

That day the Falconers found out how the International Crew made their living. It came up during an extended breakfast of Meg's pancakes that lasted all morning and had several seatings. Pretty soon, Teebs was sent out to buy more Bisquick, and then again when they ran out of syrup. It was like a party, complete with jokes and laughter and good-natured ribbing.

The only pooper, Meg reflected, was Aiden. He sulked at the table, leaving his stack untouched on his plate. And not once did he pass up a chance to take Meg aside and lecture her on the dangers of getting too chummy with the gang members.

"I'm having *fun*," she whispered. "Remember fun? Or have you always been a sad sack?"

"Meg – they're counterfeiters!" He filled her in on the details of his brief but intense encounter with Zapp in the bathroom.

"Well, it's just Zapp," she said sharply. "Viv told

me exactly what they do. They're like couriers. They make pickups and drop-offs for people."

"Criminals," Aiden amended.

"But not counterfeiters. It's mostly gambling stuff. Numbers, they call it."

"And that's not illegal?" Aiden challenged.

"So what if it is?" she said defensively. "Compared to what you hear about big city gangs these days—"

She was interrupted by a commotion at the front door. Bo had arrived along with two other IC members, and they were a sight to behold. They were battered but triumphant, their clothing ripped and crimson-stained. Congratulations and high fives were flying in all directions, and Meg couldn't help noticing that the knuckles of Bo's right hand were dripping blood all over the carpet.

"What happened?"

Bo favoured her with a goatee-framed grin. "We made a statement."

"What statement? You're bleeding!"

"Remember the guy with the knife? Well, forget him."

Meg's eyes were like saucers. "You mean he's—" Aiden delivered a sharp kick to the back of her ankle. "Is he all right?" she amended.

"That depends on the talents of the Emergency Room personnel." Bo peeled off his tattered, bloody T-shirt and tossed it into a scorched metal wastebasket. He passed it to his two companions, who did the same with their blood-spattered shirts.

Meg watched in wonder as one of Bo's companions squirted lighter fluid on top of the shirts and produced a book of matches.

"Not in here," Viv ordered. "I'm not washing any more black soot off the ceiling."

Meg turned even paler. Of all the International Crew, she felt closest to Viv. Viv was like a big sister, removed, somehow, from the uglier aspects of the IC. But it was pretty plain that the girl was in it up to her ears.

Meg heard a match strike outside, followed by the *foom* of an accelerated fire. She moved a step closer to her brother.

Bo noticed her distress. "It's nothing for you to worry about," he said kindly. "Just a little difference of opinion. We made a few pickups the Furies thought were theirs."

"The Furies?" she repeated. "Are they another —" Aiden kicked her again — "autonomous collective?"

Bo laughed. "No, they're a gang. They couldn't

64

even pronounce autonomous collective. Hey, what's this? You've got pancakes?"

And pretty soon they were all sitting around the table, singing the praises of Erica Graham and her magic Bisquick. From pancakes to destroying evidence and back to pancakes in sixty seconds.

Is Aiden right? Are we risking our lives being with these people?

Bo clapped his hand on to Aiden's shoulder. "You're quiet today, Gary. Something on your mind?"

Aiden set his jaw. "Just thanks and goodbye," he said with firm determination. "It's time for us to move on."

"You can stay as long as you want," Viv offered. "Right, Bo?"

But Aiden was adamant. After breakfast, they said their goodbyes, and Teebs drove them back to Venice Beach.

"Whatever you want to say about the IC," Meg commented as the big old car disappeared in a cloud of burned oil, "we could do worse than staying in that house. It's got to be the last place on earth the FBI would ever look."

"Come on, Meg – they're gang members. For all

we know, Bo killed that guy today."

Meg was bitter. "According to the newspapers, Mom and Dad are the worst criminals going. You and I are probably charged with more stuff than the IC."

"We're lucky to be out of there," Aiden insisted. "In case you haven't noticed, they're in the middle of a war. When the Furies come for payback, they could be carrying Uzis! A fat lot of help we'd be to our parents if we got caught in the crossfire."

Meg was silent. In her mind, there were different degrees of bad. *Whatever Bo did today counts as self-defence. That other guy tried to kill him.*

But she had to agree with her brother on one thing: Mom and Dad were all that mattered. Finding Frank Lindenauer was all that mattered. Bisquick pancakes and shady friends were fairly low on the list.

The first order of business was to get a hotel.

"Just a normal place," Aiden ordered. "We don't need hot bubbling mud wraps."

They went back to @*leaves.net* and reserved a room in nearby Marina del Rey using Louise Graham's SkyPoints.

Aiden replaced his sister at the screen and did a Google search for the initials "SMRC". To his dismay, the search engine spat back more than seven thousand hits. These included the Sun Marketing Resource Centre, the Scottish Motor Racing Club, and a site dedicated to the video game Super Mario Royal Castle.

"It's a dead end," Meg groaned. "It would take years to check the key against all this stuff."

"Don't be so quick to give up," Aiden advised. "We can rule out most of these right away. Look – a video game can't have lockers. And I doubt this key is from Scotland."

"How do you know?" his sister countered. "There was stuff from all over the world in that shoebox. The CIA travels everywhere."

It went back and forth like that – an argument over every item on the list. An hour later, they were at number forty-seven – the Sarasota Model Railroad Club – and Aiden looked every bit as discouraged as Meg felt.

To make matters worse, an obnoxious neighbour arrived at the next computer. This was a knuckle-cracking, under-his-breath-humming fat guy with a huge cowboy hat. He wished them "Howdy!" and plopped a gym bag on to the counter, crowding their space.

"Mister, would you mind moving that over a little?" Meg requested politely.

The man was slurping his tea so loudly that he didn't even hear her.

Meg found herself staring at the gym bag, reading and rereading the words printed on the side.

Why is that name so familiar? I've never been to California before...

And then she had the answer. "Aiden — health clubs have lockers, right?"

"I guess so," he mumbled absently, concentrating on the Google list. "Why?"

"Look!"

He followed her gaze to the duffel: Santa Monica Racquet Club.

SMRC.

Out on the street, Meg could hardly contain her excitement. "What happens now? Where's Santa Monica?"

"Hold your horses," Aiden cautioned. "Let's check into our hotel first and maybe buy some new clothes. We don't want the racquet club guys to smell us coming. If we look like runaways, the cops will pick us up for sure."

Getting around was a problem. Although Los Angeles was a big city, there was no subway, and the bus lines were confusing. Taxis were the best answer, but they were hard to find and also expensive. Aiden patted his pocket where the counterfeit fifty-dollar bill Zapp had forced on him now resided.

Phony money. Dirty money.

At first he had vowed not to spend one cent of it, to find some church or homeless shelter and give it away. But cash meant survival. And survival meant a chance to help Mom and Dad.

Whatever it takes.

But he couldn't bring himself to be grateful to a counterfeiter.

The thought had barely crossed his mind when he glanced to his left and spotted none other than Zapp himself, open for business in the shadows of an alley. He was with a "customer", handing over one of the packets of fifties, taking real money in return.

Aiden grabbed Meg, lowered his head, and chugged right on past.

"Gary!"

Zapp was behind him in an instant, spinning him around. "What are you, some kind of cop? Why are you following me?"

"I'm not!" Aiden defended himself. "Teebs drove us back to town—"

"Teebs is *here*?" Zapp's narrow weasely face had turned deathly pale.

"It was a couple of hours ago," Meg supplied. "He just gave us a lift. He didn't hang around."

Zapp nodded, absorbing the information, breathing hard. "I don't want to see you two around here any more. Got it? This neighbourhood is off-limits to you."

"OK, fine," Aiden agreed. "We're just looking for a taxi so we can get to our new place."

"You're leaving?" Zapp queried.

"Yeah," Meg jumped in. "We said goodbye to Viv and Bo and the others this morning."

"I'll give you a ride," Zapp decided.

"Oh, that's no problem—" Aiden began. The last thing he wanted was for anybody from the IC to know where to find them.

"Forget it. You're coming with me. It's not a favour, genius. I just want to see you off my turf."

Zapp drove a brand-new Infiniti G-35. He loaded up his passengers and headed south to the La Quinta Inn, Marina del Rey.

He was amazed when he heard the destination.

"A hotel? Who *are* you guys? You're not tourists!"

Aiden and Meg made no reply. Soon they'd be out of Zapp's unwanted company.

The ride to Marina del Rey took ten stony, awkward minutes. Zapp drove aggressively, pouncing from tailgate to tailgate, until they reached the circular drive of the La Quinta. He pulled over before turning in.

"Why are we stopping?" asked Meg.

"Who are you – really?" Zapp asked again. "Why do the police want you?"

Meg answered with another question. "What makes you think that?"

"It doesn't matter," said Aiden. "We can walk from here."

"Suit yourself," Zapp shrugged. "I hear the cops are nice to kids. You might get ice cream."

Aiden stared. "There's no police in there!" But with growing dread he realized that a criminal like Zapp would probably have a nose for the law.

"You don't see a whole lot of full-size domestic sedans in this part of town," Zapp explained. "There are five of them parked in that driveway."

Meg exploded. "That doesn't mean—"

And then a familiar larger-than-life figure stepped

out of the lobby. Even from a distance, Aiden could see he was a head taller than the other people moving in and out of the front door of the hotel.

The star of the Falconers' nightmares, past, present and future.

Agent Emmanuel Harris of the FBI.

11

"What did I tell you?" Zapp commented. "That's king-size heat."

Meg dropped to the floor of the back seat.

Aiden folded his long legs and tried to burrow into the space under the glove compartment. "Get us out of here!" he rasped.

"Can't. That Explorer's blocking the way. Uh-oh—"

"What?" hissed Aiden. "What's going on?"

"The big cop's coming this way." Zapp honked at the SUV and rolled down the window. "Hey, move out!"

"Shhhh!" pleaded Meg, pulling a rain shell off the seat to cover herself.

Pressed in between the floor mat and the glove box, Aiden began to tremble. Sure, he was hidden from normal view. But not if Harris walked right up to the Infiniti. "Listen – that guy's an FBI agent.

If he finds us, you think he isn't going to search this car? Drive on the sidewalk if you have to!"

Zapp's voice was tense. "Don't you think that might attract a little attention at a hotel full of cops?"

"Yeah, but—"

"Shut up!" breathed Zapp. "He's right here!"

Aiden and Meg cowered in terror. Not since their parents' trial had they been this close to the man who had destroyed the Falconer family. His presence still had the power to paralyse them.

So this is how it ends, Aiden thought numbly. *Caught hiding like scared rabbits. And another promotion for J. Edgar Giraffe.*

Zapp had a death grip on the steering wheel. He sat frozen, staring straight ahead.

And then Harris was looming over them. He was so big that he actually blocked out the sun, his bulk casting a shadow over the interior of the car.

The earth seemed to stop on its axis. No one spoke.

The sun came out again.

"He walked right past us!" Zapp whispered. He craned his neck. "He's going into the Starbucks down the block!"

In one fluid instant, the SUV drove away, and the

Infiniti leaped back into traffic. Zapp stomped on the accelerator, and the La Quinta was soon half a mile behind them.

The Falconers crept from their hiding places. No sooner had Aiden resumed his seat than Zapp's fist snapped out and caught him on the side of the head. Aiden saw stars.

"Hey!" Meg practically climbed over the centre console, but a straight-arm from the driver pushed her back again.

"You bring the feds down on me? Knowing what I've got in this car?"

"We were going to take a cab!" Meg raged. "You *made* us come with you!"

"That's the only reason you won't be washing up on the beach tomorrow morning!" Zapp growled. "You tell me, and tell me now, what the FBI wants with a couple of snots like you!"

Aiden's head was still ringing from the blow – the gang member had a jab like a pile driver. He clung to one thought through the pain: *a busted face is still better than capture.*

Meg was angry enough to go toe-to-toe with Zapp. "We're not telling you squat! If you lay a hand on either of us, I'll rat you out to Bo, *you and your little side job*!"

Aiden could see Zapp's knuckles whitening on the steering wheel, could feel red-hot anger bubbling just below the surface. His little sister was the bravest person he knew, but she was playing with fire. Danger from Zapp could be a whole lot worse than danger from Harris.

Aiden had a horrible suspicion that washing up on the beach was more than just a colourful figure of speech.

It took the driver a long time to calm down. When he finally spoke, his voice was merely a snarl. "You think Bo is like a big purple dinosaur who loves everybody. You don't have a clue."

"Bo likes us," Meg shot back.

"He won't be running things for ever."

By unspoken agreement, Zapp drove the Falconers back to the little house owned by the Department of Veterans Affairs.

When Viv asked about the nasty and fresh-looking bruise on the side of Aiden's head, he replied, "I hit myself with the car door. Clumsy."

This earned an approving nod from Zapp.

Aiden climbed the stairs with an ice bag for his head, and Meg went with him. When the door closed behind them, Meg posed the one question that had gone unspoken during the roller-coaster ride of the day's events: "How did J. Edgar Giraffe know what hotel we'd be going to?"

"Easy," Aiden concluded wearily. "He must have figured out what we've been doing with Mom's frequent-flier miles. No more free hotels, Meg."

She nodded. "Good thing we've got this place."

"Yeah, great," Aiden told her. "We've got front row seats at an autonomous collective of psychos."

"Not true," she told him angrily. "Most of them are really nice people who made some bad choices because they weren't as lucky as us."

"Right," Aiden said sarcastically. "I thank my lucky stars every night."

"We grew up in a real home with fantastic parents who loved us. The IC kids – they went totally apewire over instant pancakes! How pathetic is that?"

"Don't shed any tears for Zapp. That guy's all the way bad. We didn't escape Hairless Joe just to get mixed up with someone who's even worse. I don't think we're *safe* here."

"Maybe," said his sister. "But I know we're not safe anywhere else."

Aiden had no choice but to agree. With Mom's SkyPoints now out of reach for ever, even the cheapest hotel would dry up their money in a heart-beat. They'd be out on the street in this big, tough, strange city, where their mugshots were pinned to the bulletin boards of every police station in town.

We'd be totally exposed.

The memory of quaking in the shadow of Agent Emmanuel Harris was something that would haunt him for the rest of his life.

The Santa Monica Racquet Club had its own building – a modern, ultra-hip glass and gunmetal structure in the middle of a long street of glass and
gunmetal.

This was the high-rent district. Meg felt self-
conscious in the thrift shop clothing she and Aiden
had bought that morning. At least she was allowed
to be a girl again. But with denim shorts, a white
T-shirt, and hair that was only beginning to grow
back, she looked like a plain kid, gender unspeci-
fied.

Aiden gazed bleakly at the front desk and its
MEMBERS ONLY sign, plainly visible from the street.
"How am I ever going to get to the locker room? A
snooty place like this has a dozen personal trainers
per square foot. They kick you out if you're not at
least a movie producer."

Meg was disgusted. "After all we've been through,

you're afraid to sneak past a couple of muscle heads? Watch me. You'll know what to do."

She marched into the building and up to the granite counter. A barrel-chested man in a tank top and a badge that declared him to be Chad fixed her with a dubious stare. "Is there something I can do for you, kid?"

Meg looked wan and worried, and swayed a little. "I don't feel so good. . ."

Aiden watched in amazement as Meg's legs gave way under her and she started to crumple. Three weightlifters were out from behind the desk to catch her before she hit the floor.

The performance was so mesmerizing that he almost forgot to act. At the last second, he scooted past the drama and down the sumptuously carpeted corridor. He dashed between a double row of glassed-in squash courts and came to the men's locker room. With a sigh of relief, he slipped inside.

It was tough to make a sweaty changing room posh, but the club had managed it with elegant tile work, marble shower stalls, and framed sports art on the walls. The lockers were a burnished bronze and glowed, unscuffed and perfect.

Aiden followed the numbers: 345 . . . 346 . . . 347.

An ordinary padlock hung there. Fingers trembling, he took Frank Lindenauer's key from his pocket and reached for the lock.

"No fooling!" came a voice behind him. "We've been taking bets on when somebody was actually going to crack that thing."

Aiden wheeled around to face the speaker, who regarded him in surprise. "That's *your* locker?" the man said. "When's the last time you came in here? Kindergarten?"

"It's – my dad's," Aiden stammered, wishing he had his sister's gift of gab. "I haven't had the guts to empty it since the accident." *Not bad – eat your heart out, Meg.*

The man looked embarrassed and escaped to the showers.

The moment of truth. Aiden inserted the gold-coloured key.

A perfect fit!

He turned it and felt the tumblers fall into place. The lock clicked open and the door swung wide.

In that instant, he knew a different kind of fear – not fear of capture or of harm. The contents of this locker were their last clue, their only lead.

What if it turns out to be a dead end?

There was only a single item on the bottom shelf — a thick manila envelope, unsealed but fastened with the metal clip. Aiden scooped it up and headed for the exit.

As he strode through the lobby, he caught a glimpse of his sister, propped up against the counter, being tended to by a whole lot of muscle.

She nibbled at a power bar while Chad lectured her: "In the warmer weather, it's important to guard against dehydration and replenish electrolytes."

As Aiden hustled by, she leaped to her feet. "I feel better now. Thanks, guys." She was hot on his heels.

The instinct to flee was so much a part of them now that they had sprinted three blocks before it occurred to both of them that Chad and his army of personal trainers were not going to put out an APB over a couple of nuisance kids.

They found a small park and sat down under a tree. Aiden undid the clip and pulled out the documents they hoped could save their parents.

They stared in dismay. The envelope held a stack of printed leaflets, meant to be folded in three. They advertised an organization called the East Asian Children's Charitable Fund.

"I don't get it," Meg mused. "He's a CIA agent, not a charity worker."

"There's an address," Aiden noted, "and a phone number."

But further investigation shed no light on what Lindenauer was doing with pamphlets from an overseas charity. At a payphone, Aiden learned that the number had been disconnected. Information had no current listing for the East Asian Children's Charitable Fund. They bought an LA city map only to find that there was no such street as Dersingham Road.

Meg was grasping at straws. "Maybe Frank Lindenauer is a nice guy. Mom and Dad liked him, right? Maybe he donates money to East Asian children."

"Not through this charity," Aiden retorted. "It doesn't exist."

Meg frowned. "Can a charity go out of business?"

Aiden didn't answer. He was staring across the park, his face white as a ghost.

Meg was alarmed. "What is it?" She followed his gaze, fully expecting to see Emmanuel Harris and a team of officers advancing on them. But her brother's gaze was fixed on the plywood fence around a storefront that was under renovation. Its surface was completely covered with ads and hand-bills.

As if in a daze, Aiden got up and began to cross the park towards it.

No, he thought. *Impossible. I'm hallucinating.*

Meg followed, still nagging. "What's going on? What do you see?"

Then she spotted it, too. At the centre of the collage of posters and bills was a large close-up picture of a man with thick red hair and a heavy beard.

"It can't be!" Meg whispered, awestruck.

Aiden took the nine-year-old photograph out of his pocket. There could be no doubt that this was the same person.

Why was there a picture of Frank Lindenauer right out there on the street?

The Falconers goggled at the poster of the one man who could prove their parents' innocence. Over the orange-brown of his beard, bold letters asked:

DO YOU KNOW THIS MAN?
Call (310) 555-2120

"I can't believe it!" Aiden breathed. "We've been hunting this guy across the country and back again! And now he's looking out at us from a wall? It's – it's like the Twilight Zone!"

Meg was jubilant. "Well, what are we waiting for? We know this man! Call the number!"

They tore down the poster and headed back to the payphone.

Meg had to do the dialling. Aiden was so keyed up, he required both hands just to hang on to the receiver.

Could this be the end of our quest? And not just ours

— a team of lawyers couldn't find Frank Lindenauer! Could it really happen this way — with Frank Lindenauer finding us?

A man's voice answered on the first ring: "West Hollywood Rehab Centre."

"Uh — hello," Aiden stammered. "I saw your poster. I — I think that's my — uh — uncle. Where is he? What happened to him?"

"The John Doe on our flyers is suffering from severe amnesia," was the reply. "Our doctors feel that the familiar faces of family and friends might jog his memory. I'm not permitted to give out any more information over the phone."

Meg, who was huddled up to the receiver to hear what was being said, began to jump up and down with excitement. "That's why he didn't come forward!" she hissed. "That's why he couldn't testify at the trial!"

Aiden shoved her away. "Well — uh — can I see him? He might recognize me." *Better not to mention that the last time I met Uncle Frank, I was six.*

"Not without the doctor. He begins his rounds at ten o'clock. Would you like to make an appointment for tomorrow?"

"No!" Aiden exclaimed suddenly. "No appointment!" He juggled the receiver back into its cradle.

"Are you nuts?" cried Meg. "Yes, we want an appointment! This is what we've been *praying* for!"

Aiden grabbed her by the shoulders. "Calm down. Of course we're going. But I don't want to make an appointment in case it's a trap."

"A *trap*?" Meg was shocked. "How could it be a trap? That's the guy – the same one in our picture!"

"Stop hollering and think!" Aiden urged. "The cops were in Aunt Jane's apartment in Boston. She used to be Lindenauer's girlfriend. They could have got a picture from her."

Meg was horrified. "You think J. Edgar Giraffe is behind this?"

"Probably not. At least, I hope not. But just to be on the safe side, let's not let anybody know where we're going to be, and when we're going to be there."

"We can't turn our backs on this!" Meg protested. "This is the closest we've ever been!"

"We're not turning our backs on anything," he soothed. "We'll sneak in and make sure Lindenauer is really there. If he is, *then* we can start talking to doctors."

Meg looked haunted. "I can't handle this, Aiden. Maybe it's the answer to everything, and maybe we're right back to square one. I can get used to the running; I can even get used to being scared all the time. But I can't wait till tomorrow to know about this!"

"Shhh," her brother cautioned. "People are looking at us. Let's walk." He folded the Lindenauer poster together with one of the flyers from locker 347 and jammed them into his back pocket. He tossed the manila envelope with the rest of its contents into a trash bin.

"I know it's hard, Meg, but we need to think this one out. If Lindenauer's been there since before the trial, he's not going to recover, be released, and disappear before tomorrow."

Meg had another concern. "What if it's the right guy, but his amnesia's so bad that he'll *never* remember Mom and Dad?"

"That's a chance we'll have to take. He's our only hope – *if* it's really him."

Meg hated riding the bus, which was slow, hot and smelly. But Aiden insisted that they had to save their taxi money. If West Hollywood Rehab turned out to be a trap, a quick, unplanned departure might be the difference between freedom and capture.

Please, God, don't let it be a trap! Meg thought.

It seemed legit enough. The posters were in quite

a few other places – bus shelters, store windows, telephone poles.

That makes sense, right? If the rehab centre wants to identify him, they'd splash his picture all over town.

Her brother sat beside her, the city map spread out on his lap. The bus routes were superimposed, colour coded, on top of the street grid. The whole thing looked like a circuit diagram of a nuclear trigger. Einstein himself would probably go cross-eyed trying to figure it out.

Meg curled her lip. That meant Aiden was going to love it. He could build a working toaster from scrap for a science fair project, but he couldn't brown a slice of bread without setting off the smoke alarm.

He finished plotting their course, then folded up the map. Perfectly. He was the only person Meg knew who could do that, too.

"OK," he told her. "We take this bus to Washington Avenue, get on the V-14 eastbound, and transfer to the C-3 into Culver City."

"If you say so." She yawned. Another thing about the bus – it was so *boring*! It was like watching grass grow – or like watching Aiden make up his mind about something – whichever was slower.

You look at the passengers; nothing to see. You look out the window; nothing to—

With a gasp, she hit the floor, pulling Aiden down with her. Two rows behind them, a middle-aged woman clucked disapprovingly.

"Meg – what the——"

His sister led him to the seat across the aisle and peered over the top of it through the smeared glass. "Look!" she squeaked. "But don't let him see you!"

The bus was waiting at a stoplight. There on a busy corner stood Zapp, deep in conversation with another teenager.

"Big deal," said Aiden. "He wants us to stay away from the spot where he does business, but that can't mean we're banned from the whole city of LA."

"Look who he's with!" she insisted.

Aiden wouldn't have recognized him at all had it not been for the Dodgers jersey. The Falconers stared at him, taking in the two black eyes, bandaged nose, neck brace and the cast on his left arm.

This was the boy who had tried to stab Bo on Venice Beach. He was still alive, but Bo's "statement" was very much in evidence.

"What's Zapp doing with *that* guy?"

Aiden and Meg watched stealthily as the IC member and the battered Fury exchanged an elaborate handshake followed by a backslapping hug.

The bus pulled away, leaving the siblings open-mouthed.

Aiden reseated himself, holding his head. "I don't think I can take any more surprises today."

"Bad enough he's a criminal," Meg seethed. "Now he's a traitor, too! When that Furies kid tried to stab Bo – it was a set-up! And Zapp was behind it!"

Aiden nodded gravely. "Remember what he said in the car yesterday? 'Bo won't be running things for ever.' I guess he meant it."

"He wants to get rid of Bo so he can turn the IC into counterfeiters," Meg said bitterly. "Well, he won't get away with it. Wait till we tell Bo!"

Aiden was alarmed. "Hold on, Meg. This is none of our business."

She stared at him. "Are you crazy? This isn't some schoolyard argument! These people play for keeps! If we let this go, Bo could wind up dead!"

Aiden sighed wearily. "You saw that guy – Bo plays for keeps, too. Yes, he's been good to us. But this is the life he chose. He knows things like this happen sometimes."

She was distraught. "Listen to yourself, Aiden! You're talking about people getting *murdered*."

"I'm glad you appreciate how serious it is," he said sternly. "You and I are babies in diapers compared to these LA gangs. In a million years we couldn't hope to understand how things work with them. If we do nothing, Bo might get hurt. But if we warn him, did you ever think about what that means for Zapp? We could turn an argument into an all-out war between the Furies and the IC! What's the body count then?"

Meg was almost in tears. "So we do nothing." Her tone was hollow.

"Wrong. We do something. We find Frank Lindenauer. We might have found him already."

He was right, as usual. Justice for their parents could be less than twenty-four hours away, in a rehab centre in West Hollywood. Starting trouble with the IC could only put their goal at risk.

Eyes on the prize, Meg, she reminded herself. *Nothing's more important than helping Mom and Dad.*

But it hurt a lot to stand idle while fate crept up on a friend.

The International Crew sat in the small living room, their eyes focused on the TV they'd inherited with the house. The cable had been off for months, and the screen showed nothing but static.

Aiden stood over the set, a picture of concentration, wrapping aluminium foil around a makeshift antenna of interlocking coat hangers.

"This isn't going to work," announced Viv. "How could it work?"

All at once, the snowy image resolved itself into the wilderness and the tents of *Survivor*.

The applause was deafening.

"Where'd you learn that trick?" rumbled Zapp.

Aiden shrugged. The fact was, he had learned it in juvenile prison at Sunnydale Farm. There had been only one ancient TV for eighteen boys, and getting reception in rural Nebraska had been raised to the level of fine art.

Bo favoured him with a goatee-framed grin.

"That's the second time you've saved my life, Gary."

The compliment stung. Saving Bo's life again, *really*, was within Aiden's grasp.

And I can't do it.

One look at Meg's long face told him she was feeling it, too.

"This show rocks," enthused Teebs. "You form alliances, act like everything's cool, and then you stab the other guy in the back!"

Meg stood up and headed for the stairs, her face averted.

"Are you OK?" called Viv.

Aiden could see Bo's eyebrows rising as Meg left the room. "I think she's just tired," he said, making a lame excuse for his sister. "I'll talk to her." He followed her up.

In their room, Aiden faced her seriously. "Come on, don't blow it. Everything you feel is written on your face."

"It's just hard, that's all," his sister murmured, "to sit there smiling when people's lives are on the line."

"Meg, we've been through this." He fell silent. Someone was climbing the stairs.

Anxiously, she whispered the name that was on both their minds. "Zapp?" If he had somehow spotted them on the bus earlier, they would be in grave danger.

But when the door swung wide, it was Bo who stood there. He stepped inside.

"I know what's eating you."

Aiden took a step back. "You do?" Could the gang leader already know about Zapp's plan? Was he about to accuse them of selling him out by their silence?

From his pocket, Bo produced a folded newspaper clipping and spread it in front of them.

Aiden saw the pictures first, their now-famous mugshots from Sunnydale. The headline read:

TRAITORS' KIDS IN LA, SAY FEDS

"That's you, right? Aiden and Margaret?"

She hung her head. "Meg."

Bo whistled through his teeth. "See, I always knew there was something up with you two. But this – man, the Falconers! The whole world heard about your folks."

Meg was belligerent. "Well, this is something you didn't hear: they're innocent. And we're going to prove it."

"You've got a lot of cops after you," Bo observed.

"Feds. Juvie. LAPD says you escaped from a full airport lockdown. You must be tougher than you look."

"What we are is desperate," Aiden admitted. "If we can't stay free, we can't clear our parents."

"It's going to get harder," Bo informed them solemnly. "The feds put a twenty-five-thousand-dollar bounty on your heads." He pointed to the third paragraph. "'For any information leading to the apprehension of Aiden and/or Margaret Falconer', yada, yada, yada. Standard cop lingo."

Aiden and Meg exchanged an agonized glance. By offering a twenty-five-thousand-dollar reward, Agent Harris had just made the entire population of Los Angeles his deputies. Now they weren't safe with anybody, anywhere.

For all we know, we're not even safe with Bo, Aiden thought.

The gang leader read his mind. "No, man, you don't have to worry about me. I meant what I said about you saving my life. I've got your back."

"Thanks, Bo." Aiden could feel his sister's eyes on him. *Tell him,* they pleaded. *Warn him about Zapp.* He turned away, unable to face her.

"Don't let anybody know who you really are," Bo went on. "You hear me? Not even the crew. Not even Viv. They like you, but twenty-five K is a lot of cash. You're lucky — you've got a place to lie low for a couple of weeks."

"We can't!" blurted Meg. "We have to be somewhere tomorrow!"

"There's too much heat," Bo insisted. "This article is from today's paper. Give waste management a chance to get your picture off people's coffee tables."

Aiden struggled to explain. "There's a guy we have to see. He might be able to help our parents. But he's in — a place. We have to go to him. He can't come to us."

Bo looked suspicious. "Are you sure this isn't some kind of cop trick? It doesn't sound kosher to me."

Aiden smiled weakly. "We're not sure of anything except this: we have to go."

Directly below the open bedroom window, Zapp leaned against the stucco wall, smoking a cigarette.

He was smiling a twenty-five-thousand-dollar smile.

It was after three a.m. when Agent Emmanuel Harris entered the police station.

"This better not be a false alarm," he growled.

"Sorry to get you out of bed," the night lieutenant apologized as he escorted the FBI agent to the interrogation room, "but I think this guy's for real. He knew that your kids are going by the name Graham. That wasn't in the papers."

Harris increased his pace, and the lieutenant had to scramble to keep up. "What did he say about them? Are they OK?"

"Just that he knows where they are, not another word. He's a real piece of work, this one. Even for around here."

"Criminal record?"

"Not yet. But it's in the mail, that's for sure." He opened the door to reveal a slight, greasy-haired youth in the logo-clad gold chain uniform of a West Coast gang member. "Meet Maurice Zapp, one of Pocatello, Idaho's, most prominent citizens."

Harris thought he saw recognition in Zapp's cold eyes. Did that mean that this lowlife — and possibly the Falconers — had been close by and watching him?

Zapp got right to the point. "When do I see the cash?"

Harris had been alive for more than forty years, and never had he taken the kind of instant dislike to anyone that he had to this scruffy teen. "When I see

Aiden and Margaret Falconer," he said with distaste. "Where are they?"

"Relax, jumbo," Zapp advised. "They're in a safe place. Give me your mobile number. I'll call to tell you when and where to grab them up."

Harris leaned over menacingly. "That's not acceptable. I don't have to let you walk out of here, you know. Wasting a peace officer's time is public mischief."

Zapp was not intimidated. He smiled sweetly up at the hulking FBI agent. "You want those kids or what?"

15

Meg peered out the grimy window as the bus lumbered east through Beverly Hills en route to West Hollywood.

Wilshire Boulevard . . . Rodeo Drive. . .

These were famous streets. Tourists came here from all over the world. The Falconers had planned a family vacation in California. Dad had even bought airline tickets.

And then an FBI battering ram had come smashing through the front door.

Plans, she thought bitterly. Other families got to make plans. They tooled through these neighbourhoods in rented convertibles, following maps of movie stars' homes, oohing and aahing over dreamland mansions.

While we pass by it all on a smelly bus, scared out of our wits, not knowing if today's the day we save our parents or the day we get caught.

She took in the sights through the scratchy lenses

of her cheap sunglasses. That was the disguise of the day – sunglasses and Lakers caps, farewell gifts from Bo. The crew leader had been up with the sun to present them. "It's not the time to be waving your faces all over town," he had told them.

The poor guy doesn't even know he's in as much danger as we are.

Aiden's attention was riveted to the oncoming street signs, his face carved from granite beneath his shades. His cautious nature usually got on Meg's nerves. But right now she was comforted to note that her brother was taking this with dead seriousness. It was their first shot at Frank Lindenauer. Possibly the only one they'd ever get.

Aiden pressed the button, signalling their stop. "This is us."

The bus lurched to a halt. Aiden and Meg stepped into the California sun in a daze. It wasn't the uncertainty or even the danger that shook them. It was the sheer *importance* of this trip.

"Playing for all the marbles" was one of their father's favourite expressions.

Well, Dad, we're shooting for the marble mother lode today.

They headed south on foot until they spied a red-brick building that stood out among the pastel colours of its neighbours. It reminded Meg of a smaller version of her elementary school – low and rectangular, practical but boring. A sign declared it to be the West Hollywood Rehabilitation Centre.

Could the answer to their prayers be waiting for them inside those dreary walls?

Bo paced a groove in the already worn carpet of the living room. This was stupid. Why was he stressing out on behalf of two kids he didn't really know and who had refused his advice? It wasn't as if he didn't have anything else to occupy his mind. This dispute with the Furies – he had almost got knifed over it. And it wasn't going to get any better until both sides started talking.

And yet his mind kept slipping back to the Falconers. Poor kids. Bo had always known they were runaways. But their true identity, what had happened to their family—

There were a lot of hard-luck stories on the streets of LA, but theirs was in a league of its own. It didn't make any difference whether the parents really were innocent. Who wouldn't root for Aiden and Meg, knowing what they were up against and how far they'd come? Busting out of Juvie, outsmarting airport security, making the feds look like monkeys. . .

It was the stuff of street legend. There was only one problem: the street was no place for a couple of clean-cut kids.

His eyes fell on the elaborate contraption Aiden had rigged as a TV antenna so they could watch the evening news tonight. Bo wished he wasn't so sure Aiden and Meg were going to be on it, captured or worse.

I should have gone with them, he thought.

They probably would have said no. They wouldn't even tell him where they were going or who they were meeting there.

Viv came down the stairs, unfolding a large piece of paper. "What do you make of this? Gary and Erica must have left it."

The two spread the poster on the coffee table in front of them. It was a close-up photograph of a bearded red-haired adult, captioned DO YOU KNOW THIS MAN? He vaguely remembered seeing these around town, although he had paid them little attention. He didn't recognize the guy.

Was this the person the Falconers had gone to meet?

Frowning, Bo flipped open his mobile and dialled the number. A male voice answered almost immediately. "West Hollywood Rehab Centre."

"I'm calling about your poster," said Bo. "I think I might know the dude."

There was a pause. Then, "Thank you very much. The man's family has already been located." Click.

It was a brush-off, no question about it. He dialled information. "West Hollywood Rehab Centre, please." Bo listened to the number. It did not match the one on the poster.

Aiden and Meg were walking into a trap.

"Get your shoes on," he told Viv. "The kids need our help."

"What's wrong?"

"That's what we have to find out." He marched into the kitchen where Teebs and Zapp were scraping smouldering lumps of blackened Bisquick batter from the frying pan.

"We never should have let the squirt leave," Teebs was complaining. "She's the only one who can get it right."

"Where's West Hollywood Rehab?" Bo cut in.

"Isn't that on Cascadden, just off Wilshire?" asked Teebs.

"We've got to get over there," the leader ordered. "Now."

Zapp regarded him questioningly. "Gary and Erica?"

"They're jammed up," said Bo. "And I owe them."

Teebs and Zapp abandoned the ruined pan. "I'll take my own car," Zapp tossed over his shoulder. "Meet you there."

As he stepped through the front door, he was already dialling his mobile.

The West Hollywood Rehabilitation Centre wasn't crawling with cops, and there were no police cruisers parked outside or circling the block. Taking a page from Zapp's book, Aiden even checked for full-size domestic sedans. Nothing. The coast was clear.

Still, he was nervous. *The problem with traps is that you don't know they're traps until it's too late.*

There was a reception desk. No security guard. It was a busy place, like a miniature hospital. Doctors, nurses, staffers, patients and visitors bustled in all directions.

"OK," Aiden told Meg, "just walk right in like you know where you're going."

"Shouldn't we just ask to see the guy on the posters?" asked Meg.

"Then they'll know it's *us*," Aiden told her. "If it's a trap, that's as good as knocking on Agent Harris's office door. The place isn't huge – how many rooms can it have? Maybe we can catch a glimpse of the guy."

The automatic doors slid wide and they stepped inside, striding briskly but without obvious hurry. Aiden sensed dozens of pairs of eyes on them.

Stop shaking, he ordered himself. *You're just paranoid because those mugshots were in yesterday's paper.*

With effort, he pushed the feeling from his mind.

"We did it," Meg whispered when the lobby was out of sight behind them.

Aiden nodded breathlessly, pondering their next step. Two kids walking into a place like this looked like regular visitors. But two kids wandering the halls, peering in doors, was another matter. Pretty soon, some nurse or orderly might wonder why this pair looked so familiar.

We've got to get this over with quickly.

"We'll split up," he decided. "I'll check the upstairs, you take the main floor."

"And if we see Frank Lindenauer?" she prompted.

"Then we'll find each other and go straight to the front desk. If he's here, we've got nothing to worry about. But if he isn't, the sooner we're out of this place, the better."

The upstairs was laid out more as a hotel than a hospital, with long hallways flanked by numbered rooms on both sides. This, Aiden guessed, was where the rehab centre's patients lived, leaving the ground level for doctors' offices and medical facilities.

The first door was open, and he poked his head inside. A small space, neat and spare, with a single bed. It was empty.

"Looking for someone?"

He was startled back out into the hall. A young nurse was regarding him.

"My – uncle," he managed. "I don't know what room he's in."

She pointed down the corridor. "Ask at the nurses' station. They can help you." She disappeared into the stairwell.

Aiden let out a long breath and peered into the next door.

"There you are!" cried a high-pitched, quavering voice. "I thought you were coming yesterday!"

The grey-haired woman who appeared was so tiny that Aiden very nearly missed seeing her. She was quite simply the shortest, smallest adult he had ever laid eyes on. A clawlike hand, delicate yet at the same time powerful, closed on his arm. "Come and sit down. Did you bring your guitar? You know how I enjoy it when we sing together."

Aiden was at a loss. "I – I think you've got me mixed up with somebody else."

"Nonsense, dear. You're Jonathan from the high school. Did you honestly think I could forget my favourite visitor?"

"I'm not Jonathan," Aiden said earnestly. The mini-person looked so crestfallen that he added, "But I'm sure he'll be here any minute."

"Why don't we play cribbage?" The little lady pushed a chair over to her closet, climbed up, and began rummaging around the top shelf. Her perch teetered dangerously.

Aiden froze in the act of sneaking out the door, then rushed to her side. "Please come down, ma'am. If you need something, I'll get it for you."

"Oh – lovely. Thank you." She stepped gingerly to the floor. "We'll need the cribbage board, and a deck of cards, of course. And while you're up there, Jonathan dear, could you look for my crochet bag? I haven't seen it in months. I'll never finish that table-cloth if I don't get to it, you know. . ."

Up on the chair, Aiden began to do battle with a collection of belongings crammed into the top shelf under pressure. *If this ever lets go,* he thought, *I'm going to be pinned to the far wall.*

Meg would strangle him if she could see him now. The clock was ticking, and he hadn't even begun searching because he was afraid to offend a tiny person with a lot to say.

Meg scoured the cafeteria for a face to match the one on the posters.

Nothing.

Her unease was on the rise. If Frank Lindenauer wasn't in the building, that meant Aiden was right.

I hate it when Aiden is right.

She didn't even want to think about what that would mean – that she and her brother were not the hunters but the hunted, and they had walked into hostile territory.

Quit whining! she ordered herself. *You're getting to be as bad as Aiden. For all you know, he's sitting upstairs with Lindenauer this very minute.*

The rehab centre, which had seemed fairly small from the street, turned out to be deep, extending all the way to the next block. On the main floor alone, there was a cafeteria, a full gym and weightlifting facility, an indoor pool with Jacuzzi, a modest library, and dozens of therapy cubicles.

Back out in the hall, she continued to work her way towards the rear of the building. The rooms here reminded her of doctors' offices, with medicine cabinets and padded exam tables. Meg had to stand on tiptoe at each door, peering in the glass through angled venetian blinds.

I look like a Peeping Tom, she reflected. How was she ever going to explain herself if somebody came along?

Then she saw it: between the thick slats at the window of room 41 – shoulder-length hair, very full. Dark reddish-brown, just the colour of—

Heart thumping, she burst through the door. "Uncle Frank!"

A young red-haired woman in a surgical gown was perched on the table while a doctor examined her knee.

"What do you want?" barked the doctor. His eyes narrowed at the youngster in the low-brimmed cap and dark shades. "Who are you? What are you doing here?"

A dozen glib excuses popped into Meg's head, but her silver tongue let her down. It was the "Who are you?" that did it. It was not a fugitive-friendly question. She fled without a word. She was so flustered that she ran headlong into a burly orderly. The collision sent her staggering backwards, stunned. The sunglasses hit the floor beside her.

And then she and the big man recognized each other.

Oh, my God—

The horror swelled, clogging her throat, making it difficult to breathe. Of the many dangers that competed for equal time in Meg's nightmares, this was the one she thought she'd left back east in the twisted metal of a wrecked Hummer.

The burn from an erupting air bag was still raw on the bald man's forehead.

The orderly was Hairless Joe.

17

Neck muscles bulging, the mysterious assassin reached for Meg.

The jagged bolt of terror that sizzled through her body jolted her into a split-second reaction that probably saved her life. She hurled herself down the corridor in a full sprint. Hairless Joe was right behind her, closing the gap with each stride of his powerful legs.

Her high-stepping sneaker narrowly missed a lunch trolley standing by the wall. Pivoting like a ballerina, she whirled around and kicked the obstacle into her pursuer's path. The cart upended right in front of Hairless Joe, depositing its cargo of meal trays on the floor. The assassin hurdled athletically over the trolley, but his foot slipped in a mound of creamed spinach, sending him crashing heavily to the linoleum.

Meg kept on running, grudging herself the

delay of a quick glance over her shoulder. A single thought flashed through her mind, eclipsing all others.

Find Aiden.

For all her frailty and slight stature, Mrs Enid Metcalfe was a force of nature. This was the fourth time Aiden had tried to finesse his way out the door only to be drawn back into a conversation about the late Mr Metcalfe, Cousin Gertrude, assorted nieces and nephews and the beastly woman who had run her down with a grocery cart at Winn-Dixie.

"Not only did I break my hip," she complained, "but I haven't seen my hearing aid since."

Light dawned on Aiden. *No wonder she doesn't hear me when I tell her I have to leave.*

"I'll come back and see you soon!" he all but bellowed, and made a determined exit. It would be up to the real Jonathan to make good on that promise.

He had just started down the hall when Meg erupted from the stairwell, wide-eyed like a cornered animal.

"What happened?"

She grabbed him by the arm, threw open the

nearest door, and hauled him inside – right back into Mrs Metcalfe's room.

"No," he hissed. He'd never be able to explain how hard it had been to escape from here the first time.

"There you are, Jonathan," the old lady was saying. "I looked up from my crocheting and you were gone. And who's this lovely young girl?"

Meg grasped their hostess's narrow shoulders. "You've got to hide us!"

Mrs Metcalfe was mystified. "Hide you? Whatever for?"

"Is it Harris?" Aiden demanded. "It's Harris, right?"

"It's Hairless Joe!"

The name was like a body blow, knocking the wind out of him.

Hairless Joe? Here? But how?

The answer was frighteningly simple. If the bald assassin could find them in Vermont and Massachusetts, he could find them in California. There were ways – news reports of the chase at the LA airport, the frequent-flier miles—

Aiden dropped to his knees, pulling Meg down with him. The two scrambled under the bed.

"Do you happen to see a silver brooch down there, Jonathan?" Mrs Metcalfe asked. "In the shape of Rex Harrison's hat from *My Fair Lady*—"

Aiden cut her off. "If a big bald guy knocks on the door, don't let him in, OK? He's dangerous."

"Like that woman at Winn-Dixie!" she exclaimed.

Aiden pressed his face to the carpet, his pulse hammering in his ears. Hairless Joe. No one else conjured up such instant, unreasoning terror. Even Emmanuel Harris, the Falconer family's arch-enemy, was an FBI agent – a real person with a real job. You understood what he was doing and why.

But Hairless Joe was a killer without a name.

We can't even figure out why he wants us dead!

It was like being stalked by a wild beast. No – worse. An animal acted on ancient instincts; Hairless Joe was an intelligent predator – cold, calculating, professional.

And the only thing between him and us is the world's smallest blabbermouth.

Aiden fought to see beyond his panic, but he found only despair surrounding it. Even if they somehow managed to escape the bald assassin once again, then what? The posters were a trap, just as he'd feared. No Frank Lindenauer. They were right back where they'd started.

How could it be worse?

His thoughts were interrupted by a sharp rap at the door.

"Don't answer it!" rasped Aiden.

"Go away!" called Mrs Metcalfe.

The latch clicked, and Aiden could feel a breeze from the hall. He fought down an impulse to run out and protect their tiny hostess.

Don't be stupid! She's got a whole lot less to be afraid of than you do.

"Young man, get out of here at once or I'll call security!"

"Take it easy, lady, I saw them come in here."

Wait a minute, that's not Hairless Joe! That sounds more like—

The Falconers scrambled out from under the bed.

"Bo!" Aiden exclaimed. "What are you doing here?"

"I came to warn you this place is a trap, but I see you already figured that out." He cast his goatee-framed grin in the direction of Mrs Metcalfe.

"Nice bodyguard. I guess the ex-wrestlers were all busy."

Not a ghost of a smile from either sibling.

"It's no joke, Bo," Meg quavered. "The guy after us is a cold-blooded murderer!"

Bo looked surprised. "What – you mean he's *here*? In the building?"

"I barely got away from him!" she exclaimed.

"What's his beef with a couple of kids?"

"We don't know!" Aiden answered. "He followed us all the way across the country – he's already tried to kill us twice!"

Bo took the practical approach. "Calm down. Teebs and Viv are outside in the car. Just stay close to me, and you'll be fine."

Strange but true, thought Aiden as they ventured out of the room. He was relieved to have Bo on the scene. *He may be a criminal, but he's exactly the kind of guy you need to handle Hairless Joe.*

Still, he wondered if even a streetwise LA gang leader could be a match for a professional killer.

They started down the stairs, with Aiden and Meg glued to the IC leader's sides.

"Chill out," he told them. "It's not a three-legged race."

An orderly appeared on the lower landing, and

Meg nearly jumped out of her skin. Her reaction triggered Aiden's startle reflex. But it was just an ordinary employee, not their enemy.

He's out there somewhere, though — around any corner, behind any door, watching and waiting...

They reached the main floor and headed for the entrance. Aiden allowed himself to breathe a little easier. The lobby was a busy place. Surely, not even Hairless Joe would risk attacking them in front of a dozen witnesses.

His sense of comfort lasted about three seconds. For there, at the front desk, towered the six feet seven inches of Agent Emmanuel Harris, holding the Sunnydale mugshots out to the receptionist.

As a single person, the Falconers twirled away from Bo and began walking hurriedly in the opposite direction.

Surprised, Bo rushed to catch up. "Now what?"

"That big guy at the desk," whispered Aiden. "He's FBI."

Bo whistled under his breath. "You guys are like the king and queen at homecoming. Everybody wants a piece of you."

"This guy wants all the pieces," Meg amended bitterly. "And he wants them in jail."

"Hey!" Harris said suddenly.

Aiden's blood frosted over in his arteries. He risked a backward glance, his body coiled like a spring, ready for full flight.

Behind them, the FBI man had called over a nurse to look at the photographs.

False alarm.

Bo grabbed their wrists and yanked them back into the stairwell, out of view.

"That was close," panted Meg as they ran up the steps.

"We've got to get out of here," Aiden urged. "Sooner or later he's going to show those pictures to somebody who's seen us."

"There has to be another exit," the IC leader said determinedly.

"Not from the second floor," Meg pointed out.

"We'll get as far from reception as we can up here," Bo decided. "Then we can look for another way down."

They strode past Mrs Metcalfe's room, past the nurse's station, and turned down the long hall that led to the rear of the building. Their eyes fell on the rear stairwell at the end of the corridor. All three broke into a run.

Aiden got there first. He reached for the handle just as the heavy metal door swung open and a figure in pale blue scrubs stepped out.

Hairless Joe.

The shock wave travelled from Aiden to Hairless Joe, to Meg, and finally to Bo. The assassin was the first to react. With a well-practised windmill motion, he reached into his elastic waistband and pulled out a pistol. A black cylinder was attached to the end of the barrel.

A silencer.

He's going to shoot us right here in the open! Aiden thought, petrified.

The weapon swung around until it was pointed at Aiden's chest.

With a battle cry, the leader of the International Crew flung himself at the bald man just as he squeezed the trigger. The pistol fired – a sound closer to a cough than a gunshot. Aiden felt the bullet whiz past his shoulder, missing him by an inch or less. It tore a small chunk out of the door frame behind him.

Viciously, Hairless Joe slammed the butt of the revolver into Bo's head. The gang leader crumpled to the floor, out cold.

"Bo!" Meg cried. Desperately, she grabbed the

first thing she could get her hands on – a rolling cart bearing a portable heart defibrillator. With all her might, she swung the heavy device, sending it wheeling towards the assassin.

It curved around and struck his elbow. The gun dropped from his hand and skittered across the floor. Hairless Joe dived for it, his hand reaching for the grip. Meg's foot came out of nowhere, stomping on his outstretched fingers. The bald man howled in pain.

"Aiden, help me!" She gasped, grinding her sneaker down with all her might.

But Aiden's slack-jawed attention was focused not on the battle on the linoleum, but on the battery metre on the defibrillator. It read full power.

As he took the paddles from the cradle, there was a high-pitched whistle like a camera flash recharging itself. "Get off him!" he ordered Meg.

"No!" she cried, horrified.

There was no time for an explanation. Aiden reared back his foot and delivered a swift kick to his sister's hip, sending her sprawling. His hand now free, Hairless Joe picked up the pistol.

And then Aiden pressed both paddles on to the assassin's bald head.

19

With a click and a power hum, the defibrillator pumped four hundred joules of electricity into Hairless Joe. It was enough of a shock to jump-start a stalled heart. To a healthy person, it was like being struck by lightning.

The assassin's body went rigid and jumped eight inches, knocking the paddles out of Aiden's hands and sending him sprawling. The gun fired three quick muffled shots into the suspended ceiling. Then Hairless Joe dropped like a stone and lay there, unmoving, beside Bo's unconscious form.

Meg was wide-eyed. "Is he dead?"

Aiden was practically hysterical. Hairless Joe had *meant* to kill. But was the real murderer Aiden Falconer?

His heart fluttered out of control like he had taken that shock himself. "I don't know if I can handle this," he managed, his teeth beginning to chatter.

Meg tried to reassure him. "It was self-defence! He was going to shoot us!"

It didn't change the fact that Aiden had deliberately acted to end someone's life.

His hand shaking, Aiden placed a finger lightly on the throat of the man who had nearly killed them yet again.

A pulse – faint but strong.

"He's OK!"

A groan escaped Hairless Joe's pale lips, and he tried to raise his head.

"Let's fly!" Meg picked up the gun and heaved it with all her might down the long hall. She hesitated. "Bo…"

Aiden glanced at the trickle of blood oozing a crooked line from the spot where the pistol had struck … then saw Bo start to stir. "Someone will come. He'll be fine." He threw open the stairwell door.

And froze.

Uniformed police officers were pouring up the steps, their rapid footfalls echoing in a disorganized tap dance.

"Cops!" gasped Meg.

Aiden fought to force his whirling mind to function rationally. *Harris at the entrance – LAPD on the stairs…*

They could jump out a window, but two broken ankles wouldn't make for a speedy getaway.

We're trapped!

His eyes fell on a line of folded wheelchairs leaning against the wall. The image came instantly – a slide show transmitted directly into his brain: a dark green book jacket bearing a picture of a wheelchair. Silver foil lettering declared: *Medical Malpractice: A Mac Mulvey Mystery*.

The climactic scene: Mulvey, trapped in the burning hospital, facing a fiery end. The only tool at his disposal – a wheelchair. . .

Can it work?

Aiden wasn't sure. But one thing was obvious – staying here to be arrested wasn't an option.

He looped his wrist under the armrests of two of the chairs. Then he threw open the heavy door and dragged his sister into the stairwell.

She gawked at him in utter disbelief. "No!" she hissed. "The cops—"

There was no need for her to finish that sentence. A chorus of shouted *Hey!*s attested to the fact that they'd been spotted.

A short flight led up to where a sign declared ROOF ACCESS.

They ran for it, blasting through the fire door and

out on to the flat tar-paper roof. Working with frantic haste, Aiden located the softest landing below – flower beds on high mounds of fresh topsoil. He set up the two wheelchairs eighteen inches from the edge.

Meg was beside herself. *"That's your plan? Jumping off the roof? Are you crazy?"*

Aiden shoved her into one of the chairs. "There are shock absorbers in these things! Mac Mulvey—"

"Mac Mulvey isn't real!"

Aiden seated himself and rolled right to the edge. Looking down almost cost him his breakfast. The drop seemed enormous. Thirty feet, maybe thirty-five.

We're only two storeys up. Why is it so far to the ground?

To Meg, he said, "Stand up and take a good run at it! You've got to jump clear of the front of the building!"

"I don't think I can do it," Meg whimpered. "I'm too scared!"

There was a crash as the heavy door opened and slammed against a chimney. A uniformed policeman burst out and took in the sight of the Falconers at the edge of the roof.

"Don't jump!"

Aiden and Meg lifted up the wheelchairs, took one running step, and flung themselves into thin air.

There wasn't even enough time to scream. It was like planet Earth reached up and yanked them down with merciless violence. Aiden held on to the armrests for dear life, squeezing himself into the seat as his senses blurred and the flower bed hurtled up to meet him. The wind roared in his ears. He was picking up speed – too much speed—

I've killed both of us! Sorry, Meg…

The impact jarred every cell in his body. It knocked the air out of his lungs. The wheelchair collapsed under his weight, and he wound up flat on his back in soft black soil.

Meg hit the ground an instant later. Her chair lost a wheel, but otherwise held together. She bounced once and spilled out of it, rolling in the dirt.

Aiden scrambled up and hauled her to her feet. "Alive?"

"Barely," she breathed.

There was a commotion on the roof above them. Six horrified LA cops peered down. At least three of them were shouting into walkie-talkies.

"Can you run?" asked Aiden.

Meg set her jaw. "Just watch me!"

The two sprinted down Cascadden Street. They

were rounding the corner when Agent Harris came lumbering out the main entrance. "I see them!" he barked into his handset. "They just turned west on Hillmount!"

He loped down the drive and folded himself into a rented Ford Taurus.

At that moment, Bo staggered out of the building, holding a fistful of bloody paper towels to his forehead. With a two-fingered whistle and a hand gesture, he directed the El Camino out of its parking space. Teebs stomped on the accelerator and swung the big car around. It screeched to a halt at the end of the driveway, blocking the Taurus.

Harris leaned on the horn. "Move out! Police business!"

Teebs and Viv grinned and waved and pretended the engine wouldn't start. Bo collapsed to the lawn, exhausted but triumphant.

Aiden and Meg pounded along the pavement, their minds blank of all thought except for escape. At this point, Aiden could not separate the pain of his burning chest from the injuries of his spectacular fall from the roof of the West Hollywood Rehabilitation Centre.

You're out. You're alive. Keep moving.

He pictured the LA city map that he dared not

slow down long enough to remove from his pocket. An endless grid of streets stretching scores of miles from the ocean to the desert. Hours of travel, even in a car. On foot, an impossible journey.

We have to stop sooner or later. . .

He thought of what was behind them – Agent Harris, the LA police force, Hairless Joe—

. . .but not yet.

"Don't know what you're talking about, man. I never saw any kids."

Bo sat in a treatment room in the rehab centre while a doctor placed seven stitches in the gash in his scalp. Agent Harris paced in front of him like a caged tiger, barking questions and getting no answers.

"Aiden and Margaret Falconer." He jammed the crumpled flyer with their mugshots two inches in front of Bo's nose. "Travelling as two brothers, Gary and Eric Graham."

"Doesn't ring a bell."

Harris was exasperated. "Does twenty-five grand jog your memory? That's the reward if you can help bring these kids in."

"I'm Amish."

"Be smart, Boaz. Think what you could buy with that much money. Just tell me what you know."

"I told you already – I was here visiting this old lady—"

"Whose name you don't remember," Harris finished sourly.

Bo looked up as a Steri-strip was taped over his wound. "So now it's a crime being forgetful? *I'm* the one with the busted head! Why don't you go hassle that hard-core cue ball who pistol-whipped me?"

"*What?*" Harris stopped in his tracks. "A bald guy? Describe him!"

"The kind with no hair," Bo snapped. "And a serious-looking gun with a silencer straight out of James Bond."

The agent snatched up his walkie-talkie from the table. "Janza, I need the building sealed off – *now*! We've got a white male, bald, six feet tall—"

Bo shook his head. "Don't bother. He was long gone when I came to – probably miles from here by now, walking the streets while you're rubber-hosing law-abiding citizens."

Harris was shocked into speechlessness. So the bald man had eluded him once more. Who was this mysterious assassin who always seemed to be a step ahead of the FBI?

A silencer – that was the mark of a professional.

He took a closer look at Boaz, the street tough

who definitely knew more than he let on. *This delinquent is probably the only reason the Falconer kids aren't lying dead at this crime scene.*

"Tell me one thing – what would make a guy like you take on an armed man to save a couple of strangers?"

Bo shrugged impassively. "Don't know any strangers. That's what makes them strangers." He paused to let his trademark grin bloom at the centre of his goatee. "But maybe – just maybe – one of those strangers saved my life."

The sign on the van read TOUR OF STARS' HOMES. They had already viewed palatial estates owned by Danny DeVito and Henry Winkler and had passed by the gates of Steven Spielberg's compound.

Aiden and Meg saw none of it. They had spent the first hour catching their breath and trying to calm the percussive pounding of their hearts. Their fellow passengers were blown away by the fact that Gwyneth Paltrow's pool cabana had been designed by Picasso's great-grandniece. But it was impossible to care about things like that when you had just barely escaped with your life.

"I've got to hand it to you, bro," Meg said fervently. "I thought you'd gone psycho with that wheelchair high-dive. Who knew it was going to work?"

"I asked Dad about it once," Aiden admitted. "Back when the book first came out. He said: 'How should I know? You think I'm crazy enough to try it?'"

Meg blanched. "You mean you weren't *sure*?"

"I was sure we had to get off that roof."

She regarded him with equal parts fury and admiration. Aiden the wimp, Aiden the nerd. Yet when the stakes were high – really high – he was as brave as a lion. She would probably never figure him out, but she was very glad to have him on her side.

"We should have known those posters were a trap," Aiden mourned, rubbing a bruised elbow. "That picture of Lindenauer looks exactly like the one in my pocket. Like the guy hasn't aged in nine years."

Meg nodded grudgingly. "But whose trap? The FBI's or Hairless Joe's?"

"I wish I knew," her brother said moodily. "The FBI could have got that picture, but when you think about it, so could Hairless Joe. He was at the house in Vermont. That's what really burns me up. After all we've been through, we know nothing more than we did when we first arrived in LA."

"That decorative wrought-iron gate guards the magnificent estate that once belonged to screen legend Charlie Chaplin," came the commentary over the van's PA system. "It's been said that, on nights with a full moon, you could see Mr Chaplin out here in his underwear, polishing the brass."

Meg snickered at her brother. "And you thought we didn't learn anything."

He smiled, but both of them knew that, at this moment, nothing was very funny. Nothing had been since the battering ram had annihilated their front door, a million years ago in another lifetime.

The laughs are few and far between when your family is in tatters and you're a fugitive, Meg thought dismally.

"I wonder," Aiden said with a sigh, "if Mom and Dad were right when they went on TV and told us to give it up. I mean, we're wanted by every cop in the country. And now even the people who don't hate us because we're Falconers can make a pile of money by ratting us out. It's us against the *world*, Meg. Six billion against two. We're totally alone."

"Not totally," Meg pointed out. "What about Bo?

Whatever you think about the IC, he sure proved he's on our side."

Aiden was still depressed. "He's only one person."

"Today," she reminded him, "one person on our side turned out to be enough. If it wasn't for him, we'd be dead." She turned melancholy. "And look how we repay him. We're going to blow town without even warning him that Zapp is selling him out."

Aiden looked thoughtful. "Maybe there's something we can do. . ."

The Taurus's cup holder was broken, so the coffee teetered precariously on the seat. Agent Emmanuel Harris manoeuvred through Venice Beach traffic, wondering exactly what he was doing here.

It had been pure luck that his assistant back in Washington had been checking up on Harris's voice mail.

"This is Aiden Falconer," said a shaky but determined young voice. "We're ready to turn ourselves in. Meet us at five o'clock in Venice Beach. There's an alley about five hundred feet east of the corner of Washington and Taggart. We'll be there, waiting."

Harris had listened to the message over his mobile phone at least a dozen times. His hopes were not high. He doubted that two kids who had just jumped off a roof to avoid capture would be inclined to throw in the towel and surrender themselves that very afternoon. But whatever the reason, the Falconers seemed to want him there and he had to check it out. At this point, it was his only lead, and as good a place to look for them as any.

He pulled the Taurus up to a fire hydrant — one advantage of working for the federal government was that all tickets could be fixed.

There was Taggart Street. He could see the opening to the alley up ahead. "Come on, kids," he mumbled under his breath. "Be smart." Harris knew he would never sleep soundly until Aiden and Margaret were off the street. Cutting down on the caffeine would probably also help.

The instant he stepped into the alley, he knew two things: one, that the Falconers were not going to be there. And two, that they had directed him here for a specific purpose. For there, handing over a bundle of crisp freshly printed fifty-dollar bills and accepting a handful of regular cash in return, was the unsavoury teenager who had sold the Falconers out for the reward — Maurice Zapp. No FBI agent could mistake what was going on here — the passing of counterfeit money, a federal crime.

Spying the big cop, Zapp tried to run. But Harris,

who looked clumsy, was not. He threw Zapp up against the brick wall and cuffed him on the rebound. To the cowed customer, he said, "This is your lucky day. Scram."

Zapp was outraged. "What are you arresting me for? I gave you two runaways!"

Harris nodded, half in wonder. "And they gave me a counterfeiter."

Not bad on a fugitive's busy schedule. You had to admire those Falconer kids.

Five storeys straight up, a pair of expensive opera glasses that had once belonged to Frank Lindenauer peered over the roof edge of an apartment building.

Aiden lay on his stomach, following the drama below. He watched with satisfaction as Agent Harris slapped handcuffs on Zapp and led him back to the Taurus.

Meg crouched beside him. "Is it finished?" she whispered, refusing to look for herself. Being close to the hated J. Edgar Giraffe, even for the right reasons, felt like playing with fire.

"Stay down," Aiden advised. In his opinion, the coast wouldn't be clear until Harris and Zapp were in the Taurus and the rental car was well out of the opera glasses' considerable range.

He kept the lenses trained on the sedan as it turned left on Taggart and stopped at a light. Aiden was surprised at the power of the dainty mother-of-pearl glasses. He could clearly see the rat-tail in

Zapp's greasy hair through the back window. He could even read the licence plate and make out the Avis sticker. Also the street signs at that intersection – the corner of Taggart and Harvey. And what did it say in smaller letters under Harvey? He fine-tuned the focus, and there it was:

FORMERLY WESTERN AVENUE

The notion that struck Aiden was so shocking that he nearly fumbled the glasses off the roof and came close to following them down.

Meg pulled him back from the edge. "What's wrong?"

"That street down there –" he managed, "it used to be Western Avenue!"

"So?"

He unfolded the crumpled flyer from Frank Lindenauer's locker at the Santa Monica Racquet Club – the one advertising the East Asian Children's Charitable Fund. The address was printed at the bottom:

47 DERSINGHAM ROAD

Meg was confused. "But there *is* no Dersingham Road, remember?"

"Not now. But what if it was like Western Avenue? Street names get changed all the time. What if it's something else now?"

The Falconers exited the roof the way they'd come up – by way of a dingy freight elevator that deposited them in the building's basement laundry room. A narrow hallway clogged with garbage cans led to the alley that had once been Zapp's place of business.

"Slow down!" Meg hissed. "You want to catch up to Harris?"

But Aiden was a man on a mission. Their destination was *@leaves.net*, the cyber tea shop. This time, they skipped the order counter and marched straight to a computer monitor.

It took exactly ten seconds. A Google search for keywords "Dersingham Road" led to a news release from the Los Angeles city council dated six months before:

Dersingham Road to Be Renamed
in Memory of Actor Marlon Brando

The discovery filled their sails like a blast of wind at the stern of an ocean schooner. Yes, it was only an address. But if being a fugitive had taught Aiden one thing, it was this: the difference between no clues and one clue was the difference between despair and hope.

As long as there's a lead to follow, there's still a chance to save Mom and Dad.

The taxi ride to 47 Marlon Brando Way ate up nearly all of their money. Aiden didn't have the heart to pay the driver with Zapp's counterfeit fifty.

The street was an endless row of small businesses – tattoo parlours, juice bars, joke shops and tiny ethnic restaurants. Number 47 was—

"Glatt Kosher Persian Cuisine?" Meg read off the sign announcing their grand opening. "It's supposed to be a children's charity!"

Right next door, the proprietor of Glen's Comics and Collectibles was sweeping his front steps. "You remember that, huh?" he said to Meg. "What a nightmare! Crime-scene tape all over the place, the whole building locked up by the Department of Homeland Security. They had to rename the street to get rid of the rubberneckers. Ruined my business for months!"

Meg was amazed. "Why would Homeland Security shut down a charity?"

The man shrugged. "Who knows? I'm just glad

it's over. Hope those glatt kosher Persians like comic books." He disappeared inside his shop.

"Homeland Security?" Aiden repeated. It made no sense. And yet a feeling of deep uneasiness was working its way up his spine. Homeland Security was the arm of the government that had prosecuted the case against their parents.

And then Meg pinched him so hard, he cried out. "Aiden – *look*!"

The front window had just recently been scraped of its previous lettering. Not much of the gold paint remained. But where the writing had once been, the glass was cleaner. From the right angle the words were as clear as if they had still been there:

THE EAST ASIAN CHILDREN'S CHARITABLE FUND

A PROJECT OF HGG

The world tilted. Aiden felt sick.

HGG

The name triggered the darkest memories from the darkest days of his life. The beginning of the end of everything for the Falconer family.

HGG – HORUS Global Group.

John and Louise Falconer had used their skills as

criminologists to prepare terrorist profiles to assist American agents in identifying sleeper cells. They had believed they were working for the CIA. But the Falconer profiles had ended up in the hands of HORUS Global — a front for the terrorists themselves.

Now it appeared that the East Asian Children's Charitable Fund was also a front — for HGG. Part of the same extremist organization.

And Frank Lindenauer had their flyers in his gym locker.

Meg's voice was barely a whisper. "Does this mean what I think it means?"

Aiden was numb with shock. How many thousands of hours had Mom and Dad and their lawyers spent racking their brains over what had become of Frank Lindenauer? Why hadn't he come forward during the trial? Was he sick? Dead? Had he gone insane, or lost his memory? Was he living in a shack in Iceland, away from all communication?

How could he let his friends John and Louise Falconer take this rap when a word from him would have cleared them?

Now they knew. Frank Lindenauer had never worked for the CIA. He worked for the HORUS Global Group. He was on the side of the terrorists.

Someone had indeed been guilty in the most famous treason case in the past fifty years. But it was not John and Louise Falconer.

"Uncle Frank!" Aiden spat bitterly. "He framed them, Meg! Mom and Dad are in jail because of him!"

His sister turned to face him. "I know it sounds crazy, but should we be calling the cops right now? I mean, doesn't this prove Mom and Dad are innocent?"

Aiden shook his head. "All it proves is that *Lindenauer* is guilty. And since he was their connection, it might even make the case against Mom and Dad stronger."

Meg pounded on her brother's arm in sheer frustration. "That's so unfair! We've come so far; we've almost gotten killed a dozen times! Only to make them look *guiltier*?"

Aiden had no words of comfort. "Fair" was no longer in his vocabulary.

Helplessness always made Meg angry. "Seriously, Aiden, are we trying to do something that can't be done? If the truth isn't good enough, what is?"

And there, from the depths of their despondency, Aiden snatched the answer: *we've never been looking for the truth. We know the truth.*

The object of their search wasn't truth. It was Frank Lindenauer.

A rush of purpose strengthened his will and his backbone. He almost felt exhilarated. Not *better*, precisely. In fact, the task ahead of them had become a lot harder.

But somehow knowing what you have to do makes the whole thing seem less frightening.

"Nothing's changed," he told his sister. "We're still searching for Frank Lindenauer. But it's not enough just to find him any more…"

He swallowed hard, and when he spoke again, he was amazed to hear determination and even confidence in his voice.

"Now we have to bring him in."

The chase never lets up…

ON THE RUN 4

THE STOWAWAY SOLUTION

An extract…

"Mr Bass – your son is on line two."

Mitchell Bass, the well-known Washington attorney, picked up the receiver. "Jonathan – is everything OK?"

"It's not Jonathan," declared a voice that was both shaky and determined. "It's Aiden – Falconer."

Falconer.

It was a name wrenched from the top stories of CNN. Doctors John and Louise Falconer, the husband-and-wife criminologists convicted of treason. The charge: aiding and abetting foreign terrorists.

Mitchell Bass had been their lawyer. He had tried – and failed – to prove that the Falconers had been working for the CIA.

Bass drew in a breath. Fifteen-year-old Aiden Falconer was a fugitive from justice. He and his eleven-year-old sister, Meg, had escaped from a prison farm for young offenders. They had been eluding the juvenile authorities, the FBI, and more than a dozen state and local police departments for more than two weeks.

"Aiden—" he managed. "Where are you? Is Meg with you? The FBI said you were in California—"

The voice on the phone was suddenly sharp, wary. "You talked to the FBI?"

"They called me," Bass explained. "They thought you might try to contact your parents' lawyers. Aiden, listen to me – I talked to your parents, too."

All at once, the teenager's tone softened. "How are they?"

"Worried sick," the lawyer said honestly. "They're more concerned about you two than they are about prison. Both of them begged me to convince you to turn yourselves in."

There was hesitation on the other end of the line. "Turn ourselves in. . ." Aiden mused.

"Give me that phone!" There was a brief struggle, and then an angry voice – a young girl's – declared, "No way, Mr Bass. If that's what you're thinking, forget it. The next cops we hang around will be the ones who let Mom and Dad out of jail."

"Meg," Bass said sympathetically. "Your parents are serving life sentences. We did everything we could, but—"

"You *didn't* do everything you could!" the girl

cried. "We found evidence that Frank Lindenauer worked for the terrorists! How come nobody figured that out, huh?"

Bass was stunned. "That's impossible!" Frank Lindenauer was the Falconers' CIA contact. By the time of the trial, he had flat-out vanished. How could two kids on the run have uncovered what a team of professional investigators had missed?

Aiden came back on the line. "We got into Lindenauer's old gym locker. He had a stack of flyers for a charity run by HORUS Global Group – and HORUS was a front for the terrorists."

"Remarkable!" exclaimed the attorney, making notes on a legal pad. "It could help the appeal. But you have to understand it doesn't prove anything to a judge. Just because Lindenauer may be guilty doesn't mean your parents are innocent."

"That's why we have to dig deeper," Aiden told him. "We need the information your firm gathered about HORUS."

Bass was bug-eyed. "For what?"

"To prove our parents were framed. We have to find Lindenauer. Someone from HORUS knows where he is."

"But there is no HORUS any more," Bass protested. "The FBI shut down their Denver headquarters and all their satellite offices. Everybody associated with the group is in jail."

"Frank Lindenauer is out there somewhere," Aiden pointed out. "*He's* associated with HORUS. And there's a professional killer after us—"

Bass was more worried than ever. "A killer?"

"He might just be a big, bald psycho. Or maybe some yahoo who wants revenge on our parents. But what if he was hired by HORUS to tie up the loose ends?"

"All the more reason why you have to go to the police," Bass insisted. "You're in grave danger. Not just from this threat, but in general. Think of your mother and father. Surely it can't be your plan to add to their burdens."

Despite his powers of persuasion, Bass could not convince the Falconer siblings to give themselves up. They honestly believed that they were their parents' only chance for freedom. Bass swallowed a lump in his throat, torn between admiring their bravery and seeing nothing but tragedy in their future.

Their safety was his number one priority. But if they refused to be saved, he had to help them any way he could. With a heavy heart, he instructed Janine, his assistant, to fax the firm's file on HORUS Global Group to the number Aiden provided.

Janine sat unmoving in her swivel chair, the thick

folder clutched to her chest. On the desk in front of her lay a copy of *The Washington Post*, open to page six. Her eyes were glued to Department of Juvenile Corrections photographs of Aiden and Margaret Falconer, and the headline above them:

$25,000 REWARD OFFERED FOR CAPTURE
OF FALCONER SIBLINGS